1957

THE
LIVELY ARTS
OF SISTER GERVAISE

the
LIVELY ARTS
of
SISTER GERVAISE

by

JOHN L. BONN, S.J.

P. J. KENEDY & SONS
NEW YORK

Library of Congress Catalog Card Number: 57-6668
Copyright © 1957 by P. J. Kenedy & Sons, New York
PRINTED IN THE UNITED STATES OF AMERICA

THE
LIVELY ARTS
OF SISTER GERVAISE

Chapter 1

Sɪsᴛᴇʀ Gᴇʀᴠᴀɪsᴇ sat down at last. Anyhow, the play had been a success.

From where she was hidden in the darkness of the stage she could hear Mr. MacGill, the custodian, sweeping up the mimeographed programs that Sister Drusilda had made for her in the bursar's office, and the cigarette butts of which Reverend Mother disapproved. They littered what tonight had been the lobby of her theatre and tomorrow would be the corridor to the gym.

She hoped he got everything up, but now she would not think about that. Not even about the girls, noisy in 3-B or the boys shouting in classroom 3-A. Let them dress. Give them time. These moments were her own. She would not even worry about Rosemary Morrison and Joe Maguire. Nor Father Cooney, the pastor. She would just wait.

She had switched off all but the pilot light, and the strong, acrid odor of dying floods was around her. She liked the smell, the lumpy feeling of the divan they had got from the St. Vincent de Paul Society when Mrs. Morrison had refused them her best front-room set. She liked the expanding silence after the show.

Nobody needed to say it. She knew. The show had been good. But what a struggle! Worth it, though. They had produced an excellent show. She had to admit it to herself.

Theresa Doyle's voice rose up from below. Theresa she had always with her, had chosen her from grade school years before because her voice carried. It certainly did! Perhaps, Sister Gervaise thought, I should go down and quell something. But she had been quelling things for so long that it scarcely seemed worth while any more. The last one she had quelled had been Mr. MacGill and the first one had been Father Cooney.

She would stay here. The pilot light came down like a straight finger. It would be a good effect on a single face, like Sir Henry Irving in the tomb scene from *Romeo*. But she would never be doing the tomb scene. Who did she think she was, Margaret Webster?

But, despite everything, things had gone smoothly tonight. Just that one little incident with the pop bottle, but nobody had noticed that except herself, sitting in the darkness of the balcony, far away from the stage.

When she had first come out here she had remained backstage, getting in everyone's way, raising her blood pressure. Nowadays she scurried to the balcony, unable to do anything, leaving it all to the students. Miles away above them, willing them into words, willing the audience into laughter and silence and applause. The way her father had done when he was directing. Only he was in professional theatre. She had this borderland. She had never wanted it. Mother Bernardine gave her her Obedience and shipped her off to Catholic School of the Theatre, C.S.T. She remembered what she had wanted to say:

"If my father had been a ditchdigger instead of an actor, would you expect me to be able to dig ditches? Just because he is in the theatre! Why do you suppose I became a nun?

4 ☞

I didn't want to be in show business. I wanted to say my prayers."

By now, over in the darkened convent, they had said their prayers and gone to bed while she sat here on this makeshift stage because she had never raised the objections she had considered. She had packed her toothbrush and had gone East to C.S.T. Her father had been charmed; his daughter, despite the fact that she had entered a convent, was carrying on his traditions. But he didn't understand. He was still doing rather mature leading roles, while she was here on a platform in a gymnasium. And now Father Cooney thought she was crazy, full of arty enthusiasms. He didn't like plays.

He probably had excellent reasons. The shows they had put on before she took charge had had lots of people in them. They helped to pay off the parish debt. People liked them. But this play—Ghéon. Who would go to Ghéon?

But they had come. A full hall. It had been a financial success—and that was the touchstone. The audience would come back for others. She just knew it—she thought. She smiled in a friendly way toward the uneven rows of seats. Sometimes she loved audiences. Sometimes she even loved actors. She loved . . .

Sister Gervaise laughed.

She remembered how, when she had been tired, sick of the whole thing, someone would say, "But you love it!"

How angry she used to get. But she had learned. Of course she loved it. That was the trouble. All enthusiasm, all attention, too much time away from prayer. Someday prayer might seem like a distraction. Not yet. But she was afraid. She would never mistake this for reality, this half-world. She looked through the dimness, remembering the fight for every inch.

"If you were building a football field you would give the players a gridiron, wouldn't you? But this platform . . ."

The hardwood floors into which no one was allowed to drive a nail.

"We use scenery nowadays. How am I to hold it up?"

She used sandbags, with imminent peril of a tall building's collapse. The audience waited for it, hoped for it, as they had when the quay swayed back and forth in *The Rising of the Moon*. She shuddered.

Then the other things.

Father Cooney: "All right, all right. But I don't see why you can't do a minstrel. We always did, and the Knights of Columbus loved it."

Mother Bernardine: "These plays take up so much time! The boys and girls can't think of anything else."

None had failed yet, and maybe there was an educational value in Ghéon. More, perhaps, than they got in the classroom.

Mrs. Morrison: "The rehearsals run so late. Rosemary wasn't home till eleven-thirty."

Rosemary—and Joe Maguire. The rehearsal had ended at ten. Where had they gone? By the way, where were they now? Must look into it.

Sister Gervaise rose just as Mr. MacGill barked his shins on the steps she had wangled from the Scenic Arts in Milwaukee. He began to explode but Sister Gervaise rustled.

"Anybody there?"

"Just me." She stood up. The pencil of light caught her side face. Joan of Arc. A muscle in her throat tried to raise her head up into the spot, but she controlled it.

Mr. MacGill switched on the overheads and the white light was cruel to the jumble of circled wires, one broken

6 ☞

vase, three overalls, the battered furniture badly stacked, ham sandwiches bitten into, Nick Collasanto's costume, and her precious script book. Mr. MacGill saw everything.

"Quite a mess."

She had no retort.

"When'll they clean up?"

"Tomorrow. I asked the boys for nine." That meant ten, ten-thirty. She had asked Father Rolfe, the assistant, to have the truck by eleven.

"You mean I gotta work Satidy? Look, Sister, it's getting on twelve already. I got a wife and kids . . ."

"I know. I could let myself in tomorrow if I had a key."

"Why don'tcha?"

"I don't know," she answered honestly. Months ago she had asked Father Rolfe for a key. Since then she hadn't wanted to be a nuisance and he hadn't got around to it. But there had been the night when she had left her Little Office behind and had to teach Joe Maguire to jimmy a window. Not Nick Collasanto.

"Sister! Sister!" From downstairs there was a peremptory call. It was the wasp voice of Theresa Doyle. Sister Gervaise went over to the perilous iron stairs, which were her fault. She had insisted they put them in. Otherwise they had no way of getting backstage except down the fire escape. Sometimes it had been cold.

"Yes. Just a minute!" She turned to the custodian. "Why don't you run along? I'll lock up. You don't need a key just to slam the doors."

He waved his hand toward the auditorium. "How about them things?"

Twelve hundred folding chairs, no longer in rows, and the seating cards Sister Drusilda had taken such care over, crumpled, fallen off, heelmarks on them. And down there, somewhere, the pop bottle that had rolled down the center aisle.

"I'll take care of everything, somehow." The call came again from downstairs. "Yes! Yes!"

Mr. MacGill had worn her down. He had the answer he wanted. "O.K., Sister. It's all yours."

It certainly was. "Thank you." What was she thanking him for? He hovered, but he was nearer the door, wasn't he? If he wanted to go home, why didn't he make a start?

She had to say something. "How did you like the play?"

"All right, what I saw of it. But you take them minstrels we used to have. Ever think of them?"

She knew all the answers about the sacredness of the Cause. She said: "Sometimes."

"No trouble putting them on. And the men used to help with the chairs."

She disappeared down the iron stairs into bedlam. It was bad from the classrooms and almost as bad at the end of the corridor where Dr. Maguire and Mr. Collasanto were smoking under the no-smoking signs. The bubbler would be full of cigarette butts, soggy and sorry, in the morning. Sister Emily would have a fit. She was so neat.

And she remembered Mother Bernardine: "You mustn't let anybody smoke in the building. That means even the parents. It's against the fire laws."

Obedience. She must do something. Then, just as she was getting up her courage, Mrs. Morrison appeared.

"Sister, please hurry Rosemary along. The buses only run till twelve."

"They must be dressed. I'll look."

8 ☞

Joe Maguire's voice led all the rest from classroom 3-A—
Sister Emily's—"I had a little drink about an hour ago . . ."
Mrs. Morrison raised her eyebrows as if she were asking,
"Culture? The Cause?" Sister Gervaise rapped on the boys'
door. She knew what would stop them. "Pipe down in
there!" But for Mrs. Morrison's benefit she said: "Gentlemen! Please!" And it did not penetrate to them and made
her feel like a whited sepulcher.

Dr. Maguire's voice was right behind her. "Want me to
stop the riot?"

"There isn't any riot. They're happy about the play." The
under-voice of her mind was asking, "What did you think
of it?"

She brushed by some parents she did not know and
squeezed into the girls' dressing room. They were still fully
clothed, costumed, except Jeanne Collins, who could always
be trusted and who had no talent at all. She was shivering
in her slip.

"Girls! Why aren't you dressed? I gave you enough time.
Haven't you got any sense?"

Theresa Doyle said demurely, "That's why we called you."
With her freckles covered with make-up, she achieved an
expression of worldly tolerance, explaining something obvious to someone not quite bright. "We haven't a single bit
of cold cream."

"You don't need cold cream to get out of your costumes.
Hurry up. See that they're hung up." She controlled herself.
"The cold cream's in the bottom of the desk—just where I
said it would be."

If the girls were like this, how about the boys? Maybe Dr.
Maguire, after all. She slipped into the corridor, almost col-

liding with Mr. Collasanto. He smiled and his curled lips made him look like his son Nick, whom she had cast as the villain because he could sneer.

"Boy, oh, boy, Sister! I was just saying to Joe, that was fun."

"Why, thank you, Mr. Collasanto."

"Yeah. You know when that pop bottle rolled down the aisle? Laugh? I thought I'd die. Funniest thing all night."

She could say *verry funny* the way the boys did. But she said: "I'm glad you enjoyed it. Nick was good, too." Perfectly straight. No sarcasm.

So that is what they would recall about the play. Remember the night the kid rolled the pop bottle down the aisle? What a laugh. That's what I go to those shows for—always something funny. Remember the time . . . ?

Mrs. Morrison broke in. "We can't wait any longer."

"I know. I just hurried them along."

The boys. Ominously quiet. "I do need you, Dr. Maguire. Can you find the boys?"

He grinned at her, lighting another cigarette from a kitchen match scraped on the tiling. "Sure thing. They're in the shower."

"That's good." From a rumbling distance she could hear them. She couldn't very well go down there. Heaven knows what condition the showers would be in. Poor Mr. MacGill.

And here came Mrs. Doyle, Theresa's mother, beaming and warmly understanding.

"Theresa's almost ready."

"Just take your time. You have a thousand things to do."

What a relief! She might even have something to say about the play. She did. She went on, "I don't know how you got those youngsters to remember all those lines."

Kind of a trick, a stunt.

10 ⌒

"Yes," Sister Gervaise smiled, "and Theresa did beautifully. They all did."

"Aren't you tired at all? You nuns always look so fresh. But there's so much work in these plays—just for one night."

"Yes, there is." So much work, she thought, retreating into classroom 3-B just as the boys came whooping down the hall, stringy hair half-dried and make-up still visible behind their ears.

"Hey, Sister! Weren't we swell? What did you think, huh? Did you see me play right through that noise? Pretty good, Sister?"

"There were moments," she said, "when I mistook you for human beings." She turned toward the girls' dressing room. Never let them get swelled heads. Then she went down the corridor again, remembering herself.

"Thanks, Dr. Maguire. Are they all rounded up?"

"Except Joe. Can't find my own. But he'll get along. I better get on home now. Will you give him this quarter—tell him to take the Lake Street car. Do you mind?"

"No indeed." She took the quarter. Where was Joe?

"Kind of proud of the boy tonight. How did you think he did?"

"Just fine. Excellently." Where was he? And what about the play? Did you see it at all, or just Joe? Just Joe, she supposed. "Good night."

The girls were nearly ready and the room was a mess. How they had managed to smear the desks with cold cream and sodden tissues was certainly a caution.

"Clean up everything . . ." she started, and gave up. "Oh, well." She would have to do most of it herself. Tonight. In case Sister Emily came here early in the morning, which she would undoubtedly do.

"Rosemary! Take that make-up off you right now." Child eyes, purple shadows that Sister Gervaise had put on, oriental lips.

"Please, Sister, let me wear it home."

"No."

When she said it like that, they believed her.

"Clean this place up." She started to give them an example and Jeanne Collins followed it. Jeanne wanted to be a nun.

It did not look quite so bad after a while. She made a mental note of the smudges that a damp cloth would erase. "Now, quick as you can—your parents are waiting. Particularly yours, Rosemary."

She whisked out the door and across into the comparative peace of the boys' dressing room. She hoped that the crunched cigarette butts had been smoked by parents. One, which she hid, had lipstick on it. She felt guilty, concealing it, as Mr. Collasanto, smile and all, came in.

"That's no job for a woman."

"Everything's my job."

"I thought you just directed plays."

"Oh?"

She wondered, as she scraped the remains of a putty nose off the blackboard, what they would call her in real show business. They had a word for it in school theatre. It was "moderator." This is what being moderator meant. Everything. And incidental things like putting on a play.

Then she yielded. She couldn't help it. She straightened up slowly, a twist of crepe hair in her hands, like a switch.

"Mr. Collasanto," she asked, "what did you think of the play?"

His voice was false. He said, "Swell, Sister," and she

looked at him until he went on. "I don't go in for this sort of stuff much. I'm just a dumb cookie, I guess. But it looked good to me."

"Maybe you would rather we put on minstrels?"

"Why don'tcha? I hate to see you do all this work, see. It don't seem worth it."

Was it? How would she ever know? She remembered the words: Cause, culture. Memory of beauty to last for life. Experience of finer things. Great minds speaking great words. Uplift of the audience. . . .

She couldn't say those things to Mr. Collasanto. Together they cleaned up the boys' dressing room. The greenroom. Classroom 3-A.

They were through. She thanked Mr. Collasanto and ran across the corridor laughing at herself. Eyes feel as if I'd been peeling onions. Stupid.

In 3-B there was one girl left. Rosemary, she supposed. But it was not Rosemary. It was Jeanne, the first dressed, still there.

"Jeanne! Why haven't you gone?"

To her amazement Jeanne raised tear-stained eyes.

"Oh, Sister, were we that rotten?"

"What do you mean?"

"You never said even one word to us."

She hadn't. It was true. And a moment ago she had wangled words out of Mr. Collasanto.

"Jeanne, we don't do anything to please people—not in art. We just make a beautiful thing. That's all. Not to cater to anybody—not director or audience or critics . . ." or pastors or superiors or parents, her mind added.

"But I did it to please you. I can't help it."

Sister Gervaise smiled. "You did please me. Very much."

≈ 13

"Was I good?"

She could not say it. Anybody else but Jeanne. "You were part of a beautiful thing. And you made me happy. Now run along."

Jeanne gone, she turned out the lights. Smelling the make-up, she was indeed back in a greenroom. No. She wasn't. This wouldn't do. Abruptly she went into the corridor, and Mrs. Morrison was there, tense.

"Rosemary?"

And Joe. Disappearing Joe.

"I'll get her."

"We missed the midnight."

"I know. Wait here."

Up the iron stairs and onto the stage again. Even the pilot light was out. One ray of moonlight crept through a chink in the burlap that covered the gymnasium windows, fancifully patterning the basketball net, as if through a web, a seine. First act of *The Tempest*. Hello, Margaret Webster. Never do *The Tempest*. And her voice called out softly, "Joe, Rosemary!"

Shadowy, fearful figures, coming down the aisle, up to the stage.

"Go downstairs to your mother, Rosemary. Joe, take this quarter for the car. Go down the fire escape. I'll talk to you in the morning. At nine."

She heard them tiptoeing. Somehow she had conspired with youth and moonlight and the hour after a triumphant performance against Mrs. Morrison. Wrong of her. Very wrong.

She groped her way to the doors and found them locked. Then back again. Listening to the silence. She was sure the Morrisons had gone. Rosemary with beaded eyes. Rosemary

14 ✍

with oriental mouth. Perhaps with her make-up streaked a little, brushed off with a telltale mark on her cheek. Then Sister Gervaise pressed the master switch and there were no more lights in the school except the weird ones like Christmas-tree bulbs over the fire escapes.

She went out, closing the last door behind her. Across the asphalt yard the convent looked small, protected, with snow like white top hats on its chimneys.

Like minstrel hats.

Chapter 2

MOTHER BERNARDINE had waited to see the lights go off in the school. Thank God, she thought, there was no dance after the play, for that meant that strange blaring noises, which nowadays they called music, would beat against the convent walls until midnight; then, for half an hour and more, car doors would slam, good-bys ring out, and auto horns, for some unaccountable reason, would toot at each other. There might, God forbid, even be a motorcycle.

Yet tonight would be no earlier, if a little bit less noisy. Sister Gervaise's actors were not emerging as rapidly as one might wish. What could they be doing, she wondered. What did one do after these plays that took up so much time?

Tomorrow, she knew, she would have the usual complaints. Sister Emily would find her room in disarray; Sister Drusilda would discover that the ticket stubs did not match the cash on hand; Sister Inez would be disturbed because there would be no one to accompany her to the dentist; and Sister Consolata would inevitably suggest that Sister Gervaise was working too hard and needed late sleeps, as if that weren't perfectly obvious to anyone.

Only old Sister Dolorosa—Mother Dolorosa, they still called her, though it was a courtesy title now—would go blandly on her way, peeling the candles in the sacristy, fill-ing the ciborium, folding the amices and purificators for the Masses next week, never stopping for a moment lest the rumor get about that she was too old to be useful and she be sent away to "rest" at St. Joseph's.

How afraid of rest they were. Never give up. Keep on going. She had seen them, aches and pains, blindness and senility, clinging on. The music sister up at the Cliffs was quite deaf by now. Was that why all her girls played so loud?

Work. Always work. They would have to cut down on something. But how often had she made this same determination? What could they cut down on? And then there were all those sympathetic people who in one breath told you the nuns were overburdened, and, in the next, asked you to do something for them which wouldn't take a minute. If anybody else told her something wouldn't take a minute, she would—she would—well, she'd probably do it for them.

But not this thing, not that letter in her room. Although it was only February, the Bishop, as usual, was planning ahead, and he wanted the St. Rita's nuns to take over his vacation school up at Father Fleury's mission. She would have to say no to that. But just how, she wondered, do you say no to a bishop?

Mustn't think about that now. Once she got started on that she would be composing letters all night. Better go to bed now. Sister Gervaise—what was keeping her? Must speak to her in the morning. Could find her own way in. Much, much too late.

Mother Bernardine glanced through the window toward the school. In front of it there was one sole car waiting; from the back, there was a boy's figure, rather furtively going down the fire escape. That was odd.

She let the window curtain drop and went into the kitchen for one last look at Lady, the dog, who as usual seemed to prefer the cold linoleum to her nice warm blanket beside the range.

"Go to bed, Lady," Mother Bernardine said. The dog replied with a little voice and a large thumping of tail but did not move. My only disobedient subject, the Superior thought. She stepped over the dog and refilled the water bowl from the faucet. Even Lady didn't like this chlorinated stuff. Wouldn't drink it unless it was ice cold.

Upstairs in her cell, with her rosary firm in her fingers, not slipping out as it often did, Mother Bernardine could not sleep until she knew that all was at peace. It was after twelve-thirty before she heard the side door open, the creak of the stairs, and the light footsteps that meant that, at last, Sister Gervaise had concluded her day.

The five-thirty bell always rang too early, but this morning it came from great distances shattering a dream that, annoyingly, could not be recalled, although it had something to do with Mr. MacGill playing the title role in *The Winslow Boy*.

Sister Gervaise had to say her morning offering twice before she was sure that it made sense; then before she realized it she had put on the guimpe, soiled from last night, and had to change it again for a fresh one. It almost made her late for Visit.

She had missed points for meditation, too, and she had to make up her own. Although usually she preferred this, thoughts simply would not come. It was not that she had distractions, either, because this morning the condition of the school after last night's play simply did not seem to matter. But she could not concentrate, and no picture would form in her imagination.

She was glad when it was time for Matins and the chanting demanded her attention. At Mass, of course, she was all right, although there did seem to be a sudden jump from the Gospel to the Sanctus—that is, during the time when you were sitting down.

Coffee at last. That was all she really needed. Now if you could only have coffee before meditation, how much better your prayer life would be. She had to wait for her coffee to cool. How the others avoided scalding themselves she never would know. Invariably they finished long before she did and had to wait for her. Sister Drusilda was the only one who would glance over at her, although Sister Emily's downcast long-suffering was perhaps the greater reproof. She finished as hastily as she could, and Reverend Mother's finger tapped the little bell.

The coffee isn't working quite so well this morning as it usually does, she thought, as she observed her scarcely ruffled bed. Must have slept like a log. Didn't stir all night. The ridiculous thought of lying down just for a moment could scarcely be rated as a temptation, but there was a more serious lingering over the idea of just pulling the sheets and coverlet back and letting the smoothing do for a making. She did nothing of the sort, of course, stripping the bed, turning the mattress, starting and ending as one was supposed to do. Maybe she was a little careless about the dusting, going over things just once with the dry mop, but there wasn't much floor space anyway; the desk, the chair, the washstand and the bed covering most of it.

At first when she had come here she had wished they had closets, the way they did in most houses. It seemed such a nuisance to go down two flights to the clothes room every time you needed something and take your folded garments out of the press. But now she was glad. It meant you could do your cell up in a jiffy. Why, when she was in the novitiate, she had taken quite a long time to get over her dislike of washing her own dishes at her own place at table. Now she did it automatically, taking the washbasin out of her drawer at table, pouring in the hot water that was sent around, washing, drying, emptying, and putting the clean plates back in their drawers.

Funny, how you got used to things. Once, when she had eaten at a restaurant, she had felt odd about having the waiter take the soiled dishes back to the kitchen for someone else to wash.

When she had first entered religion, she thought, she had felt as if she were playing a part, acting the role of a nun, consciously memorizing the new words, the new gestures. When had that stopped? What day had it been when the nun was the reality, and everything else seemed foreign? Now the stage business had taken its proper place and it was that which was the unreality.

No. She would never get used to that, though, to be putting on plays when she could be doing other things. Every time the Provincial came around she indicated that she would like to get out of it; every time the subject could be brought up with Mother Bernardine, she told her that it would be better for her to have some other assignment. But nobody would believe her.

Was it the penalty for doing something well? It wasn't pride that told her that she conducted her dramatic club well. She faced it as she faced everything, with realism. She knew her business. She did her job. If she were a cook it would be shameful if she didn't cook well, wouldn't it? But once in a while even a cook wants somebody to say that the soup was good and the roast wasn't burned. Not for the sake of the compliment. For reassurance. To know that you're not deluding yourself when you think that what you have turned out is satisfactory.

She finished dusting. Her room looked all right. Well—at least it would do. Someday she must get around to washing the window.

Oh no!

It couldn't be possible. How could she have got over there so early! But she had. Sister Emily was *returning* from the school and had seen the mess. Now how could she? She glanced at her silver watch. Very easily. Somehow she had been dawdling. Where had the time gone to, and nothing done? It was nearly eight-thirty.

If I scoot down to the Superior's room I can get ahead of Emily, she thought. So in that case, no scoot. I can't start any cleanup till nine anyway.

Deliberately she sat down at her desk. The papers to correct had piled up in the last week, and although her mind was not fully on them, she took the ones least likely to be interesting and plodded through them.

"Remedial English." I . . . see . . . a . . . cat. The . . . cat . . . sees . . . me. That's what they needed. What was it Nick Collasanto had said when they put him in Remedial? Oh yes. He didn't see why he needed "redeemial" English. But he could act.

"Choose the better sentence: There were a bushel of peas . . . There was a bushel of peas." According to the consensus of opinion on these papers there were certainly a bushel.

Eventually, as it was getting close to nine, she wondered if she would be summoned to the Superior's room after all. Surely some of the girls would arrive by nine. Certainly Jeanne Collins. Maybe Theresa. They would start right away on 3-B and get that cleaned up before anything else. If she went over right now . . .

Her bell rang. It was the summons to Mother Bernardine's room. Whatever Mother Bernardine would have to say, she thought on her way down, it would not come as a surprise. She did not even have to make the usual examination of conscience that usually preceded a call from Reverend Mother. She had made that. She knew what it would be about and she knew that no matter what the Superior would say, there would be an unnerving kindness in the tone. Sometimes, after you left her, it took you five or ten minutes to realize the devastating things that had been said to you.

She found herself in the room now, after only a moment or two for silent prayer at the door. Mother Bernardine smiled upon her.

"The play was beautiful, Sister."

At last she had heard it. They were good words. Funny, she thought, if I had heard them last night, it would have meant something. But now . . .

"Thank you, Mother."

"Only there are some things we must straighten out," Mother Bernardine went on. "I'm not going into them now." Her expression shifted suddenly. "You look tired."

"Oh, don't worry about me! I'm all right!" Even a horse gets tired, she thought.

"It's those late hours! You understand I realize how hard you work, but, goodness, it was almost twelve-thirty last night. But I'm sure we'll find a way. Couldn't you hurry the

22 ☞

children along at night? Then there's that smoking in the building and all that extra work for Mr. MacGill. Sometimes I wonder . . ."

I wonder, too, Sister Gervaise thought wryly, but she said nothing at all.

"I know you have your mind on so many things! I was wondering if I sent someone else over with you to, well, help chaperon while you did all those things I suppose you have to do."

"That would be fine, Mother, but . . ." Whom could she have in mind? Sister Emily?

"We'll see. Never mind that now—but—would you send Rosemary Morrison over to see me?"

"Rosemary Morrison?"

"Please."

Why Rosemary? What did Reverend Mother know? There was nothing to know. Just that she and Joe Maguire had been together for a while after the show. If there were any domestic problems she could handle them, she thought. And the worst thing you could do was to make an issue of this silly little crush. Of course, though, she would send her over.

"Certainly, Mother. As soon as she comes in."

"And I would like you to clean up Sister Emily's classroom. I don't want to have to put in any regulations about not using it."

Panic came over Sister Gervaise. Not use the classrooms? Then what could they use? What else was there? She even forgot to be disturbed about being told to do something that she was even now being delayed from doing.

"I was just going to start, Mother."

"Don't let me keep you. And see about those cigarette

stubs, won't you? I'm afraid we can't do much about the marks from them. When those fire inspectors come, they don't miss anything. Of course you do have so many things on your mind . . ."

Reverend Mother rose in dismissal. Then she turned and, with a twinkle in her eye, she said: "It's a good thing you love it."

And that was really all that Sister Gervaise could think of on her way over to the cleanup. Love it! Who gave you that idea? What put that in your head? Although all that she had said was, "Yes, Mother."

Love it, indeed!

When she reached the school, she was glad to find no girls there yet. A little physical work would help. She needed to do something.

There was plenty to be done.

In the garish light of the morning Sister Emily's classroom looked even worse than she had anticipated, and as she glanced around her eyes caught something she had not seen last night.

It was just a wisp of cloth on the floor, protruding from behind the desk. But it couldn't be! This just couldn't be!

"Oh no!" she cried.

Chapter 3

THE SCRAP OF GRAY CHIFFON that Sister Gervaise saw protruding from under the desk certainly belonged to Mrs. Morrison's dress. The one that she had promised, most unreservedly, to protect with her life. And last night she had been so sure that it was safe.

She knelt down now and pulled it out. It couldn't be! It was not only dirty, but sodden and sticky. Coke, she supposed. Must be a whole bottle of it.

For a moment she leaned back, holding the sodden mess in her hands. Then her vision cleared. Was there a cleaner in the world who could do anything with this? And it was Saturday. And whom could she trust to bring the dress to a cleaner, even if it were possible to get it done?

The thought did not enter her mind that she might find the culprits and shift the burden, making the youngsters pay for their damage. It was her responsibility, and she felt guilty, as if she were solely liable for this vandalism. Her only thought was a slight annoyance at the idea that, since she was a nun, she could not slip out with the dress to a cleaners once she had the work crew in action. She would have to get permission, secure a companion, explain everything to Mother Superior and expose the guilt of her charges —which, of course, she could never do.

There was a stirring upstairs that meant that someone was coming. Quickly she rose and put the dress into the only convenient place, Sister Emily's wastebasket, stuffing it down, putting some balls of crumpled theme papers on top of it. Nothing could harm the dress any more anyway. Then she took up a broom and began competently to sweep.

After a few moments it became obvious to her that no one intended to come down. Some nun had gone to her classroom, picked up something, and by now had probably departed. No one to help in the cleanup. It was nearly ten.

It was nearly eleven.

It was quarter past eleven.

At twenty past eleven Sister Gervaise began to feel that danger signal that she recognized and distrusted. It was not fatigue or impatience; it was, she thought, more like loneliness. She did not mind the physical work. In fact she had been rather glad to have a chance to do up classroom 3-B by herself, so that no one would know the ravages that had been made on it. But she had no key to the auditorium and could not begin that until Father Rolfe arrived. She could not do it alone anyway. Once she had tugged at the floor cloth, but it was impossible to roll it up. It would need the help of the boys.

Yet this loneliness she felt had nothing to do with the work, not even with the need of human companionship. She had spent long enough on the practice of the presence of God never to feel truly alone. This feeling that she had now came only when people had promised something and had failed to fulfill their promise. It was an experience that came oftener lately, she knew.

The teenagers did not bother to keep their word any more. They were careful enough about absolute truth, but the sense of obligation to a promise made meant nothing to them.

"I'll see you if nothing more interesting comes up," she thought. That's what they meant. Here it was, nearly half-past eleven, and she would have to be in the convent at twelve-thirty, not even in the auditorium yet, no directions given, and Mrs. Morrison's gray dress still in the wastebasket. And by the way, where was Father Rolfe, the key and the truck?

Now she had done everything that she could do by herself, and the next twenty minutes were interminable. And then everybody came at once: the truck first, and then the boys, the girls and Mrs. Morrison.

She gave all the directions. "Put the switchboard on the truck first. Get Nick to help you, Joe—and, by the way, be sure to see me this afternoon. Then pile the scenery for the Scenic Arts on top of that. Oh, hello, Rosemary. Did you finally get home? . . . Naturally we're having your mother's dress cleaned. Why, of course. Couldn't think of sending it back to her in the condition it's in, all soiled, and everything. *Jeanne Collins!* What are you doing with that wastebasket? Put it back in classroom 3-B where you found it."

Oh no! Not to the incinerator. Thanks be, she had caught that in time.

"I'm sorry. I know you were just trying to be helpful, but please do things in some sort of orderly fashion. Oh, by the way, Rosemary. Could you drop over and see Mother Bernardine? Yes, I know your mother is waiting, but I think you'd better go over just the same."

Then she could get Nick and have him take the dress to the cleaners. A boy wouldn't pay too much attention to things like that; and even if he saw the dress he wouldn't observe the condition it was in—probably. But why, when she had had all the time in the world, hadn't she taken the dress out of the wastebasket and wrapped it up? Now she would have to get it out of there furtively when no one was observing.

She managed it by sending the crew to the stage, rescuing Nick from the truck, wrapping the dress up neatly and slipping it to him. But on her way over to the convent for prayers and lunch, she panicked to see Nick leaning into the car, talking with Mrs. Morrison. Somehow or other he had managed to get her neat bundle undone, and she thought she saw a telltale piece of gray material sticking out. But it probably wasn't. Yet if there were any way for Mrs. Morrison to find out what was in that bundle, she would.

There was a note waiting for her in her napkin box. Margaret Fleming had called and would call again. She was the one who had been in love with Jimmy Dugan before he went to Korea, and though Sister Gervaise had advised them not to become engaged, they had anyway, and it seemed as if everything were going to work out all right. Jimmy was coming home soon. That must be why Margaret wanted to see her.

Mother Bernardine had not been at prayers or at lunch either. Whatever she was talking to Rosemary about was taking a long time.

After lunch Sister Gervaise deliberately slowed down her pace. There was so much to do, the whole auditorium to clean up and the chairs to stack—and that was her own fault. She should not have told Mr. MacGill not to bother. It was his duty to bother, and she had no right to burden youngsters with his job. They weren't being paid for it. But then he wasn't being paid too much either, she supposed.

Now she would go slowly. When there was a great deal

to do, it did not help to get into a tizzy. She was quite deliberate in the hallway about arranging her shawl, and when she saw Sister Drusilda, the bursar, she deliberately took the time to talk to her. She always made it a point to go out of her way to be pleasant to Sister Drusilda—to Sister Emily. There were some things on which they did not see eye to eye.

"Oh, Sister," she asked, "would you mind doing a favor for me? If Margaret Fleming calls again, would you have someone tell her to come to the convent sometime after seven? I'll be pretty well tied up until then."

"I'm going out, Sister. But I'll leave the message."

"And, oh yes! I'll try to have the bills and accounts for the play in to you by tomorrow morning."

"I'd appreciate that." Sister Drusilda looked at her meaningfully.

"I know I'm usually late with them. But I think I can manage this time."

Sister Drusilda gave her her wry smile, accompanied by a little nod of the head. It was scarcely a jovial expression or gesture. It looked, Sister Gervaise always thought, like a nod of satisfaction, such as one might make when a column of figures totaled up correctly.

Now why did I say that, Sister Gervaise wondered as she went out into the chill of the playground. Why did I commit myself to this? Isn't there enough to do to get the auditorium cleaned up—possibly to see Margaret Fleming this evening? Oh well. It's always a good idea to set a deadline. Then you really get things done. But how on earth would she get to bed by ten-thirty?

As always, the empty niche on the garden side of the school building caught her eye and bothered her. There were so many empty niches in Catholic buildings. Of course it meant only that they hadn't been filled yet, but it reminded her, somehow, of more ancient abbeys from which the statues had been removed and destroyed. Someday, she thought, I will put pressure on some group or other and have them fill that niche. She could see that statue now. It would be of Our Lady, tall and significant. And it would not have roses on its feet.

Well! Look at that now!

Whatever Mother Bernardine had said to Rosemary, it had not stopped her from seeing Joe. There were the two of them now, out on that freezing fire escape without even coats on, catching their death of cold. Those crazy youngsters! But they probably didn't even notice the weather.

She supposed that they had seen her, for they retreated almost at once into the auditorium. And now, she thought, to start that job of cleaning up the mess of place cards and pop bottles.

She was at the door when she encountered Father Cooney. He had been up there looking around, she knew. He wouldn't care about the spotless condition of classroom 3-B; all he would be interested in was the debris that must still be left in the auditorium. The gym, he would call it, taking away even her last appellation rights to it as a theatre. And if Father Rolfe had sent the truck around on time things would have been much further along.

Father Cooney's broad face beamed when he saw her. "A grand audience you had last night," he said. It was the first time he had ever been so complimentary. What was up?

"When I heard about it, I thought it was going to be one of these lives-of-the-saints things. But it wasn't bad at all. Was it by a Frenchman now?"

30 ☞

"Yes, Father—Ghéon."

"Is that so? You don't tell me. And what are you going to do next?"

"Next? That's a long way off, I hope. But I'm planning . . ."

"Sure you are. Sure you are. But you have to start something right after Lent anyway, don't you? And I was thinking, maybe we could run in something for St. Patrick's Day. You know—something musical that wouldn't take you too much time. What would you think of that now? And we could run in a little dance after it. It breaks up the Lent."

"Oh—I don't know, Father. It's quite a job. And this is February already. I don't know if I could get anything ready by March 17."

"Sister, Sister, where's your patriotism?"

Patriotism? Oh yes. She had forgotten. All priests were Irish; all nuns must be Irish, too. There were no Poles or Germans or Italians in the Catholic Church, except, of course, the Pope, and certainly, certainly no English. Besides, how could Father Cooney know her name had been Rhodes?

On St. Patrick's Day, she thought, everyone was Irish. "Why, of course it would be nice, Father. But a musical! I don't know any music."

"You don't know? But you're always after me about that liturgical stuff. I thought you were the grand musician. . . ."

"Oh, I know the scales. I know some Gregorian—and I know what's wrong. I know that much."

"What more do you need? If I can get through the preface I'm lucky. Why, you know, the thought crossed my mind to ask you to take over the children's choir. Would you consider that at all now?"

"Oh, I couldn't. I couldn't do that!" Then a thought struck her. "Unless, of course, you could get me replaced in dramatics."

"And who else would take over?" He laughed suddenly in a bursting explosion. "Drusilda? Can't you see her?"

Sister Gervaise laughed, too. The idea was ridiculous.

But then Father Cooney's face became grave. "That's the trouble with you nuns. Your pastor asks you to do something, and it's no, always. Can't you ever say yes at all? But you want me to take out 'Good Night, Sweet Jesus,' that the people love, and what will you do to replace it for me? What am I supposed to do, teach them the hymns?"

It was always like this. No matter how genially they began, it ended with an argument. Hadn't she just almost agreed to do a St. Patrick's Day show for him? She said nothing and he went on.

"But I'll tell you one thing, Sister, and that is you'll have a dance after the next show no matter what it is."

"But I can't!" she cried. "The spring play is going to be *Murder in the Cathedral!* We can't have a dance after it."

"There'll be murder in this cathedral if you don't, and I'm telling you now. You had a good crowd last night, but you can double it for two nights if you have a dance. And it's just like I was saying. It's no with you all the time."

"I didn't mean it that way, Father. It's just—just that it doesn't seem to fit in very well."

"Well, make it fit then. And by the way, will you see that those lads and lassies of yours clean up that auditorium? We can't have it left over till Monday. The CYO is meeting there tomorrow, and I don't want it left in the mess it's in."

For a moment she was furious. What did he think she was just about to do? She controlled herself. "You don't need to worry, Father. It'll be done." If you stop talking it'll be done quicker, she thought. Careful! That wasn't any way to *think* toward a priest.

She said good-by and hurried up the stairs.

Well! What was he talking about? While she had been gone the youngsters had really pitched in. The chairs were already stacked; they were sweeping the floor; and if Joe Maguire was making a Roman chariot out of Mr. MacGill's prized floor waxer, riding around on it, it couldn't do too much harm.

At the far end of the auditorium she saw a woman with a babushka on her head, dusting away as if her life depended on it. Now who could that be? Sister Gervaise crossed the auditorium and discovered Mrs. Doyle, Theresa's mother. She straightened up and smiled through the dust when she saw the nun.

"What in the world are you doing here?" Sister Gervaise asked.

The smile broadened—became more sympathetic. "Well, I'll tell you," she said. "It's Theresa's fault. She called me up and told me what a job you had, so I just thought I'd run on down and pitch in. You don't mind, do you? I bossed them all around a little."

A little? The woman must have a genius for command. There was even organization in the work.

"Mind?" she asked. "I think you're wonderful."

In her mind's eye she could see Mrs. Morrison, sitting dumpily in her car. She could hear other voices telling her to get the work done. And here was this magnificent, valiant woman—helping.

"They were all late this morning," she said. "I did get

worried that things wouldn't be finished in time. But you've done it. And they really can work, can't they?"

When they wanted to, they certainly could. Even Tommy Powers, whom she had never caught in any activity except on the baseball field, was working. And Rosemary, beautiful Rosemary, had caught the fever. Incredibly, she was sweeping.

"You are very kind," she said to Mrs. Doyle. "No one else would have thought of it."

"I'm not at all," she answered. "It's just a little gratitude. After all you've done for Theresa!"

Slowly a strange feeling came to Sister Gervaise, looking at her children there. Done so much for Theresa? So much for all of them?

Maybe, maybe she had. And it was lovely. It wasn't pride, it was just something—worth while. But it had been so long since anybody had said anything like that.

Sister Gervaise looked once more at the work in progress and at the workers, at the auditorium, even at the stage. But you love it? You love the work?

Maybe she did. Maybe they only put it wrong. Because it wasn't the work that she loved; it wasn't any *it* that she loved.

She glanced at Theresa's mother, and together they both looked out over their children.

They loved *them*.

Chapter 4

SISTER GERVAISE held her moment as long as she could. But across the auditorium she caught a glimpse of Nick Collasanto that somehow disturbed her. He had been up to something, she felt sure.

She turned and smiled once more at Mrs. Doyle and was about to excuse herself, but Mrs. Doyle anticipated her. She said, "I know you want to run along, Sister, but come on back at about four. I brought a thermos of coffee and some cake, and we can slip away and have a snack."

"Oh, thank you," Sister Gervaise said. "That—that's lovely," and sped in the direction of Nick. If only she were like Sister Emily, a little bit more! If only she had said, as Sister Emily would have, that Sisters at St. Rita's were not allowed to have little snacks with seculars without special permission. Now she would have to be clean out of the way at four o'clock. But how could you even seem to put a good-hearted soul like Mrs. Doyle in an embarrassing position? It always sounded, even when Sister Emily said things like that, like a rebuke, as if an extern ought to know the peculiarly domestic rules of the convent.

She reached Nick. He grinned at her, showing his perfect teeth, even the back ones.

"Everything O.K., S'ter."

"That's good. When did the cleaner say the dress would be ready?"

"Oh, I don't know."

"Didn't you ask him?"

"I didn't get the chance."

"Just what do you mean?"

"Nothing. Just Mrs. Morrison took it."

"She what? You did what?"

"Mrs. Morrison took it to the cleaners."

A wave of what felt almost like faintness swept over the Sister.

"You let Mrs. Morrison see that dress? After what I told you? What did I tell you to do?"

"You told me to have it cleaned, S'ter."

"Well? Did you?"

"Sure. Mrs. Morrison said she'd have it cleaned."

"I bet she did."

"Isn't that all right, S'ter?"

"No," she said. "It most emphatically isn't all right." She left Nick abruptly and scurried onto the stage. Now, it seemed to her, the youngsters were not doing their job right at all. Suddenly, she could note a hundred inefficiencies. Even the floor cloth had been rolled up before it was swept.

"Rosemary," she called, "get the boys to unwind that floor-cloth thing and . . ." She looked at it. It was too big a job. Oh, well, the dirt would come out when they unrolled it for the next play. "Never mind," she retracted. "Let it go. And come over here."

Rosemary came over gracefully and serenely. Sister Gervaise wanted to ask about Rosemary's mother's reaction to the dress, but sometimes it was better not to elicit information—better even not to know. She asked, instead, about the interview with Mother Bernardine.

"She was wonderful!"

"Was she? I'm glad. I was afraid she wasn't pleased with you about something."

"Oh no. She just told me to thank my mother for everything she had done for the convent and how she had helped, sending things over for the play—things like that."

"That's nice. We're all grateful to your mother, of course. It's been very nice of her . . ." She paused, looked at Rosemary. "Are you sure that's all Reverend Mother wanted to see you about?"

"More or less, Sister. Of course she did say something about me and Joe."

"I thought maybe. Well?"

"She was just grand. She thinks it's wonderful. So many people wouldn't understand the way she does." Was there a hint of undercurrent in that last remark?

"Just what does she understand?"

"Oh, how it's possible to go real steady with a boy and how it's all right to see him once in a while, like real often, and how you can have a real experience like being in love even if you are only sixteen."

"I see. She said all those things." It did not sound too much like Mother Bernardine. "Or did you say them?"

"Maybe I said some of them, but she agreed with me."

Yes, that was possible. Mother Bernardine's manner led you to that impression even when her ideas were quite opposed to your own. "Did she say anything else?"

"No—no. That is to say, not very much else."

"What else, Rosemary?"

"It was confidential."

Of course it was. The girl was right. Sister Gervaise knew she should not pry into a discussion between the Superior and one of the students. She hadn't meant to. She hadn't started out to do that at all. This wasn't turning out to be a very good day, was it?

"I'm sorry," she apologized. "You're quite right. I shouldn't have asked."

"But I'll tell you anyway. She said that as long as one parent approved, even though the other one didn't, it wasn't disobedience to go around with Joe."

"I see. I suppose that's right. I never thought of that before. Which one approves, Rosemary?"

"Mother. Daddy doesn't like my going steady."

"Oh. Then I should think it would work the other way—that obedience business, I mean." Wasn't the man the head of the house? Or was that being pauline and old-fashioned? And in the Morrison household it seemed improbable, even to the nun, that anyone but Mrs. Morrison could head that ménage. Besides, Mother Bernardine had said that it was all right. Or had she?

"I'm glad you got it settled anyway. But while I'm in charge of you, I don't want you scooting around with Joe the way you did last night."

"Don't you trust us?"

It was the same old question. Adam and Eve's daughters had asked it, she supposed. "It isn't whether I trust you or not," she replied. "It's whether you haven't any more sense than to trust yourself. But just remember this—I didn't do anything last night, did I? I trusted you then, didn't I? So that goes for my trust. But I don't want you to do that sort of thing again. Clear?" She deliberately changed her rather severe expression into a smile. "Even running out on fire escapes," she added.

Rosemary smiled back. "Thanks, Sister."

The hall, Sister Gervaise noted as Rosemary disappeared into the shadows, was beginning to assume an appearance of some order. Mrs. Doyle had the girls with her, dusting and rubbing down the chairs before they were piled. How long since that had been done, the nun wondered. Poor Mr. MacGill. He was a man; he could see dirt, but not dust.

Sister Gervaise crossed the auditorium, calling out orders here, encouragements there, and let herself into the little room that had served as a box office last night. Monday it would revert to a catchall for band instruments, basketballs, abandoned clothing and lost textbooks. It had to be cleaned out every time there was a show; but after the show she always cleaned it out herself, so that it was spotless. Why should that be? It didn't seem quite fair, even though she managed it by borrowing space in Sister Emily's biology cupboard. Now, she thought, she would take a few seconds to look over the bills and the accounts. They were all here— or supposed to be—in the strongbox to which she had the key. She wondered, as she riffled through them, why small bills always outdistanced her, mounting up to very large sums indeed, while large bills somehow appeared quite reasonable.

"I'm a good businesswoman," she had once said in self-appraisal. "I'm just not a very good bookkeeper." There was a difference, too. Although why she should be a good businesswoman always amazed her. She frequently made money, but she was not quite clear on how she made it. This time, if her reckonings were correct, she should have netted more than a thousand.

Netted. That was a bad word. She remembered once when Sister Drusilda had asked her, when she put in her accounts, if some figures were net or gross, and how stupid she had felt when she had had to ask what those words meant. Lately, though, she had known the difference—she thought.

Netted more than a thousand. She went over the bills and the receipts: Netted, $1,284.52.

Would she dare? If they handed the pastor a nice round check for twelve thousand dollars, wouldn't that be enough? Twelve thousand? She amended that, laughing at herself. Twelve hundred. Of course she meant twelve hundred. Then would she dare ask Reverend Mother for the $84.52 to use for a banquet for her actors and stage crew? They deserved something. You could get a nice banquet, she thought, for $84.52. Or how much did food cost nowadays? Anyway, she thought, putting the memorandum back in the strongbox, all that was left to do on this business was to make an account so that it would balance, and everything would be explained to Sister Drusilda's satisfaction.

That was not easy. She had worried once about how much you could put down for sundries. That was the word she had always used to make the accounts come out right. It represented the amount which had gone somewhere, and of which you had no possible way of keeping a record. Like the time you sent out for coffee and hamburgers for the stage crew, when they were half famished, or the tip you gave the delivery boy, or the seven yards of cheesecloth you needed suddenly in that last-minute rush. How could you remember those things? And sundries had loomed so large.

Afterward she had discovered other headings and they were very helpful. There was petty cash, now. That was a good one. Nobody, apparently, looked into that too deeply. Then there was one that she had made up herself, labeled very simply: "Clerical Disbursements." Even Sister Drusilda had been baffled by that one. Sometimes she herself was puzzled about what it could possibly mean.

Occasionally she wondered, too, if Sisters who built hospitals and ran huge institutions worked the way she did. She supposed not. In all probability they were all like Sister Drusilda.

She closed up the office, making a mental note of how much of her own rubbish she would have to clean up later, and was just about to return to the labor of restoration of the school building when she heard her name called.

No mistaking that one. It was Theresa, her voice soaring above all commotion.

Poor Theresa. She had almost forgotten about her today, and with her mother here, she had not been under foot quite so much as usual. But when Theresa called, you always had an impression of imminent catastrophe.

"Sister Gervaise!"

"I'm here in the back of the hall!"

In a moment Theresa was at her side, presenting her with the flattering incense of her adoration. "Sister," she said breathlessly, "Miss Fleming's been looking all over for you! We thought you'd got lost."

"I was doing the accounts," she said. Goodness! Why did these youngsters always imply that if you weren't visible you were—what did they call it—*fluffing off,* or avoiding them or something?

"Oh!" The tone was not exactly skeptical, but it would do. "She says she's got to find you. She says she has an appointment with you."

"At seven tonight," Sister Gervaise said. "I left word. Maybe she didn't get it."

"Shall I tell her where you are?"

There was such a dark element of conspiratorial willingness in Theresa's tone that Sister Gervaise laughed. "Why, of course, if you want to."

Theresa lingered. At last the nun said, "All right! Go and tell her. Scoot!"

"Sister . . ."

"Yes?"

"Can—can I talk to you sometime?"

"Why, of course. Any time!" She saw her every day. Whenever she turned around, Theresa was there.

"When, Sister?"

"Any time. I'm always glad to talk to you."

"O.K., Sister." Theresa disappeared.

Any time. That wasn't very good, was it? What time? Come to think of it, when had she talked to Theresa last? Really talked?

But there was no way of setting a date now. Here, very inopportunely, was Margaret Fleming.

"Come in," Sister Gervaise said, turning back to the office. "We can at least have some privacy here." If there had been any annoyance at Margaret's ill-timed arrival, it certainly did not appear. After all, if the girl wanted to see her that badly, there must be some excellent reason.

She must be very worried. One look at Margaret convinced Sister Gervaise, when she had closed the door and turned to her, that indeed she was.

"Jimmy's coming home," Margaret Fleming said. It was a flat statement.

"I know."

There was a hesitant silence then. What had happened to her? She had been such a certain little girl when she was at St. Rita's Academy. Afterward she had seemed to mature so easily through college at the Cliffs, and later, Sister Gervaise remembered the day, she had come back so proudly with Jimmy Dugan's diamond on her finger. Suppose they did have to wait a while before they were married. So what? Everybody did nowadays. She could wait.

And she had waited. And now, in a day or two, Jimmy would be home.

"I'm afraid," Margaret said.

"Afraid? You?"

This was incredible. She was a Viking type, tall and honey-haired, and when she walked it was as if she were rushing toward a cold mountain pool, crying: "Last one in is an old maid!" That, of course, was before Jimmy had gone to Korea.

"Yes. That does sound funny coming from me, doesn't it?"

"Has something happened? Has he met someone else?"

"No. It's just that he's going to."

"He's going to? Who?"

"Me." She laughed nervously. "That's crazy, of course, but it makes sense. I've changed so much. I look in the mirror and try to remember what I looked like two years ago and I can't. Not like this, though. But I can't even remember what face looked back at me then, any more than I can feel an old pain again. I just realize that there's a difference. What will he think?"

"He will think that you have matured very beautifully. You have, you know."

43

"I wonder if he will think so."

"If he's the Jimmy I remember, he will."

"But is he? I don't know that either. He's sent me pictures of himself. I have the last one over the dresser—on the mirror, you know. I look at it all the time. It's a bad snapshot of someone I never saw before."

"I see. Maybe you're really afraid more of what *you* will find."

"Both of us. Honestly. I can see him in some wild, foreign place and this stranger that I see is looking at the latest picture of me, just as I'm looking at his. He left a girl. This picture he sees is of a woman. Now he's coming back to marry this woman. And I'm the woman, marrying a man I've never seen before."

There was a rapping on the door then. Sister Gervaise shook her head at Margaret. "Never mind it," she said. "Whatever it is, this is more important." Who had told her that? Someone, some priest in a retreat. She could not remember anything but the words: No matter how busy you are, people are more important. "Go on. Keep talking to me. It won't matter what I say. My advice isn't any good, probably. The only real thing is that you talk it all out. Get it out of your system. Objectivized, isn't that the word?"

She looked around at the little office. "And while we're doing that," she went on, "you can help me straighten up this room. It's the best idea. You just talk and work and forget I'm here, if you can."

The rap sounded again, harder. No one could beat such a rhythm except Theresa.

Defeated, Sister Gervaise called out through the closed door, "Just a minute!"

The rapping ceased. But it was far more than a minute

44 ✍

before the office was put into shape, and, while they worked, Margaret told her story.

Sister Gervaise had never known exactly what had happened in the time between Margaret's college days and Jim's departure. She knew only that she had advised against their engagement, but when both of them had been so sure she had told herself that in this case it would be different. Only it hadn't been.

She could see the scenes now: the boy going off to war; the girl, a brave memory, waving a bright handkerchief, keeping the smiling mask on her face to hide the lump in her throat until at last that final vision had turned for Jim into a creased and crumpled photograph in a battered wallet. Then she saw the girl, proud and loyal, writing three times a week, waiting for the answers and showing them around.

And afterward, balanced against the impetuosity of the courtship and the suddenness of the engagement with its delightful, rebellious feeling of going against all advice, there were the months. And the very long months. And the two years.

On the other side of the world the war had stopped. The excitement, the sense of necessity, even of valor, had stopped with it. He was not fighting for Margaret now—or fighting for anything. When can I get home? And in the chaplain's office, where he went constantly, at last there was a sign over the desk, so that it was silly to ask the question any more. It read: "If you know when, tell me."

So the time had gone by and the images had grown dimmer. How much, the nun wondered, did physical love depend upon the haunting pictures in the imagination? Could she herself, she wondered, have as deep a devotion as she had, had not Christ lived on earth and had not artists, at least, perceived Him? How hard it must have been when there were no graven images.

The time had run out. "Margaret, dear," she said at last, "did you ever hear about crossing bridges when you come to them?"

"Of course."

"Well? Since you haven't even seen this new man yet and the new man hasn't seen you, I just got the funny idea that both of you might fall in love at first sight, or don't people do that any more?"

"I suppose . . ."

"You suppose too much. That's the trouble with you." She was serious now. "What you're doing is dangerous, Margaret. You keep thinking these dark thoughts and you'll make things turn out the way you fear."

"How can I help it?" She looked directly at the nun. "Of course, I know you're going to tell me to pray."

"Don't you put words in my mouth! That's the trouble with people. Just because they see us dressed up in these clothes they think they know just what we're going to say! Put a penny in the slot and out comes the nun reaction. No, you don't!"

"But don't you think prayer . . ."

"Of course I do. I do quite a lot of praying myself. But if I had said to God, 'Dear Lord, please put on a play for me,' do you know what He'd say? He'd tell me He gave me two legs and two arms and a voice and an excuse for a mind. Most of all, an imagination. He'd say, 'Go use them. Then I'll give you whatever else you need.' People *pray* too much."

"Why, Sister!"

"That's heresy and I don't mean that, but you know per-

fectly well what I do mean. They want miracles, not help."
She gave one last dab with a dustcloth. "Now you pull yourself together and start controlling your imagination and get
out of here, because I still have a thousand things to do—
including praying."

Margaret went to the door. She looks a little better, Sister
Gervaise thought, or does she? Whenever I talk to people
I think they look a little better. It's a snare and a delusion.
Maybe they do, maybe they don't.

"Ready?" she asked.

Margaret did look a little better when she smiled. "Read-
ier," she replied.

It was quite dark in the auditorium when they emerged.
Where had the time gone? There was no one left there at
all. The work had been completed and everyone had gone
home. What would Mrs. Doyle think? Sister Gervaise had
hidden out on them, leaving them to do it all themselves.
And not even a word of thanks. What a way to act!

First thing, she would get Sister Consolata to make up a
spiritual bouquet and send it over to Mrs. Doyle. The poor
kids! She would have to go out of her way next Monday to
show them how grateful she really was. The banquet!
She'd have to have the banquet.

"What were you saying, Margaret?"

She had been saying good-by gratefully. That was all.
They parted at the fire-escape door, the only certain exit
which, once closed, would secure the auditorium. Sister Gervaise went back inside and saw to it that all the other doors
were locked from within before she, too, came out on the
fire escape and slammed the door from the outside.

For a moment she stood there, breathing in the sharp February air like a long, cool drink. Her mouth tasted as if it

were full of dust. Well, it doubtless was. What was that, down there on the wall to the convent, beyond the playground? Someone waiting. A girl, she thought. Yes, it was. Now who on earth could it be?

She went down and crossed rapidly until she could make out the figure. It was Theresa. Certainly it was not unusual to find Theresa about. But what was the child doing out here in the cold? Why wasn't she home at supper? Dinner, she amended. People had dinner now. They didn't eat supper any more.

She couldn't just be waiting for her in the ritual Theresa had invented. Some time, she had feared, she would turn around abruptly and knock little Theresa Doyle's head right off. Every afternoon Theresa would walk solemnly behind her, saying nothing. At the convent door Sister Gervaise would turn and say: "Why, Theresa! How are you?" And Theresa would say, "Good afternoon, Sister." And Sister Gervaise would smile, thereby brightening Theresa's life.

But this was different. Sister Gervaise called to her as she approached, and Theresa came to her quickly.

"Thanks for waiting," the nun said. "I was tied up and I was afraid I'd missed all of you. Particularly your mother. It was just wonderful of her to help."

"Thanks, Sister." Theresa lingered. What was this, now? Oh yes. Theresa had wanted to talk. Well, she had a few minutes before Office, if she skimped on washing up.

"Why don't you come into the convent?"

"If you don't mind, I'd rather here."

"Really? Aren't you cold?" She liked the cold herself. Other people didn't.

"No, Sister. I mean—I don't mind. And I'd rather say it in the dark."

Now what had Theresa been up to? "All right. Let's walk around the grounds a little."

They walked until they came to the empty niche. Theresa had said nothing at all yet. They stopped there.

Abruptly Theresa asked, "Can a girl fifteen be in love?"

Oh, not again! Three times in one day was too much. "That depends, Theresa. You wouldn't happen to be the girl, would you?"

"Yes, Sister." She was nothing if not direct. "But I have a moral problem."

Dear me, no! Theresa Doyle mustn't have any moral problems. "What is it?"

"If you're in love with a boy and he's in love with your best friend, then it isn't right to be in love with him, is it?"

What a relief! "I don't know. You can't help being in love, you know. You just are. The only thing you can do is to control it."

"I've tried. I just can't."

"I see. Does the boy know it?"

"I don't think so. Only sometimes. Like today—the way he said hello to me . . ."

"Kind of special, was it?"

"I thought so. Only then I didn't think so. I'm all mixed up."

"Yes. You and a lot of other people. Who's the boy?"

"You won't believe me. It's awful."

"I'll believe most anything lately."

"It's Joe Maguire."

Joe and Rosemary! The one-parent approval case. "Bully for you, Theresa." Sister Gervaise cried. A great solution had come to her.

"But it's wrong, isn't it? I mean, him and Rosemary . . ."

"He and Rosemary, Theresa. And it isn't wrong. It's just right. You see, they're both youngsters. They oughtn't to 'go steady' and they're not engaged. They ought to scatter around a bit more. I know you children don't do that any more, and I'm all against this steady business. So when people aren't engaged then it's anybody's field."

"What do you mean?"

"I mean, you go right in there and fight for him, Theresa." Let Joe take a look at some other girls. Let Rosemary have a little time on her hands to discover the magnificence of Nick Collasanto's teeth. Healthier, that way.

"It's all right for me? You think I have a moral right to do that?"

"I don't think anything. I know. You just do your best. You get in there and may the best man win! I'm on your side."

"Oh, Sister, you're a honey!" Theresa threw her arms around Sister Gervaise, crumpling her wimple. It didn't matter. It must be soiled enough anyway, from the cleanup job at the auditorium.

"Honey or not," she said, "I think that's the way things ought to be at your age."

She did not say it, but Rosemary had certain advantages, she knew, considering Theresa's buck teeth. But then there were good things about not being too beautiful. If you were too beautiful, you might rely on it too much; if you weren't, you had to make up for it in personality, and sweetness and charm were, she thought, better things. "Now," she concluded, "walk me back to the convent and run home to your dinner and tell your mother she'll be hearing from me in a day or two. And after this just remember that all's fair in love and war."

At the convent door she caught one glimpse of Theresa's radiant face. For just that one moment she was beautiful—more beautiful than Rosemary.

"Good night, Theresa!"

Poor Theresa!

Chapter 5

In her cell that night after recreation Sister Gervaise realized that she had much to be grateful for. Margaret Fleming's untimely arrival had been a godsend. It had saved her the embarrassment of telling Mrs. Doyle that she couldn't drink her coffee or eat her cake, and it had left her the evening free to arrange Sister Drusilda's budget, or accounts, or whatever you called them, and she had everything neatly down in sundries, petty cash and clerical disbursements.

Also there would be no bill for the cleaners, so that the eighty-six dollars had grown to ninety. She was glad it wasn't an even hundred, because Mother might have refused her the banquet if everything came out exact like that. As it was, she had asked for a day or two to think it over, but from the look of her, Sister Gervaise was almost sure she would grant it.

Here it was, not yet ten o'clock, and she was through, done, completed. "Squared away"—that was the term for it. It had never happened before, and she felt a little bit lost, not having an insurmountable amount of work before her.

She pulled out the themes to be corrected, determining to do a few of them before she said her night prayers, but she was not concentrating really and that was not fair to the students.

She kept thinking about Theresa.

Why was it, she wondered, that one child could be so tremendously easy to influence, when you couldn't touch others at all? Rosemary now. Whatever you said flowed right off her. Margaret would come around and seek advice, which she might or might not take. But Theresa confused you with the Oracle at Delphi.

It gave you a great responsibility. She hoped that Mrs. Doyle had been right when she said that she had helped Theresa. As far as she knew, she hadn't harmed her. Yet someday a big problem would come along, and she prayed that God would give her the right words.

This wasn't the big problem yet, this schoolgirl crush. Keep it light. Keep it young. Don't let these infants get so involved. And yet there were other words for it that just might be true, and were much more beautiful. First love.

How old was Theresa now, anyway? Fifteen, hadn't she said? It didn't seem possible, but it was. Nearly five years since she had borrowed Theresa from parochial school to play the part of Jocita, the little one, in the Urban Nagle play, so that it must be almost five years ago. Theresa had been just eleven then, and it was the year after she herself had finished at the Catholic School of the Theatre. They were taking days out of the week and months out of the year lately.

Sister Gervaise put the papers aside and for a moment leaned her head against the wall. In the novitiate she would have considered this giving in to the demands of the body; now, she considered it a very sensible way of relaxing.

She remembered the first day she had met Mrs. Doyle. It

was after the play and Theresa had not recovered from the identification she had made with the Littlest Saint. It was after Mass one Sunday, and Theresa and her little brother Charlie had brought their mother over to meet the Sister.

Mrs. Doyle seemed mildly worried about Theresa. She had talked about the play and about how Theresa had "got religion" out of it. Then she had asked, "Do you think it's good for her? She's always thinking about saints and things."

And Sister Gervaise remembered how she had looked over at the children, and what she had replied to Mrs. Doyle. "What does Charlie think about all the time?"

A look of understanding came to Mrs. Doyle. She had said, "Hopalong," as if that explained everything, and Sister Gervaise shook her head yes and said, "They live in their own world. Is Theresa's world so bad?"

After that they had been friends. She had, she knew, grown quite close to Mrs. Doyle through the years. She did not see her as much as she saw Mrs. Morrison, but that was because Mrs. Morrison, as everybody knew, ran St. Rita's parish, and when she wasn't doing things for the pastor she was doing things for the nuns. She was a wonderful woman, everybody said. But for all that, Sister Gervaise liked Mrs. Doyle better.

Now Sister Gervaise remembered those other early incidents. In fact they became quite clear to her—the time she had had Theresa over for Benediction in the convent, Theresa had seen a vision, and the time when Theresa had performed a miracle, and was frightened. . . .

So clear. Almost with the vivid details of a dream. The period when Theresa had been a saint. She could see . . .

Her head fell forward and aroused her. She hadn't really been asleep. Of course not. Only two minutes had passed since she had looked at the clock last. And in those minutes Theresa had grown up, she was in high school, she was in love. Wasn't it a pity, really?

She knew Theresa so well. So well.

She leaned her head against the wall again for just a moment.

She knew all about Theresa.

Sister Gervaise certainly knew a great deal about Theresa, but there were, of course, some things that only Theresa could know about those childhood incidents of hers. She would think of them sometimes, as she was doing tonight, and a great wave of shame would come over her.

If anyone knew how foolish she had been! And one source of her gratitude to the Sister was that never by word or sign had Sister Gervaise ever referred to that business again. She would die if anyone said anything about it now. A saint. Theresa Doyle a saint!

If Joe Maguire ever knew about that! But he might have. He'd been there that day. Golly! Suppose he ever remembered it. But he'd forgotten. Maybe even Sister Gervaise had forgotten. Theresa prayed that Sister might have forgotten.

But Theresa had not forgotten. She never would. She could remember it just as clear—always. And how Sister Gervaise had snapped her out of it.

She had been eleven and she had never had a miracle. She had to have one. She had never even seen a miracle and she was eleven years old.

Her mother said she had seen it starting when Sister Gervaise had made Theresa into Jocita of Fatima, with the big kids in the high-school play, and Theresa had forgotten her freckles and barked shins and the fact that she ought to have braces on her teeth, and had gone around with a positively stained-glass expression.

Before that, she had always refused to be a lady in distress who was rescued by cowboys and had insisted on being Hopalong himself. She was the hardest-riding, quickest on the trigger, most death-defying rancher on the shores of Lake Michigan.

Then Theresa had left the world.

At first she had not known exactly how to leave the world. She had debated for a long time about taking her brother Charlie and going off to fight the Moores, but Charlie was only seven. And she could not understand why the books praised St. Theresa for wanting to fight with the Moores. The only Moores she knew were the real nice ones who always gave her raisin bread. She liked the Moores and she didn't want to fight them anyway.

Besides, the smell of the woods was a spring smell then, the odor of the sassafras dry, and the odor of the crocuses damp. So, banishing all temptations to ride herd again, and turning her back on the world, Theresa had gone to be a hermit.

She did not go too far—just to a retreat in the forests. There weren't too many forests around Wolf's Head but there were enough trees, almost, to conceal the lean-to she built. She wound the poles about with trailing pine and there was a nice green light inside until the pine dried up. She was disappointed with that, but even more so that the wild animals would not come to her.

Every hermit Sister Gervaise had told them about had had wild animals coming. That's the way it had been in the play. One of them was fed by ravens, which Theresa thought would be very pleasant. She did not like the idea of keeping a lion so much. She would have preferred a rabbit. But she ought to have something.

Theresa held popcorn out until her hand hurt. The birds hopped in chattering circles; the brown chipmunks waved their tails from a distance; a fat woodchuck whistled. But the animals were very nervous. The animals were trembling all the time.

"Look, animals," Theresa would say, "you don't have to be afraid of me. I am a holy hermit. I am going to grow up to be a saint." Sometimes she would add: "Like Sister Gervaise."

One day there was a wild thing there.

Theresa had been upset that morning. The temptation to return to the world had been very strong in her, particularly when she saw Joe Maguire's new two-gun holster. She had put out her hand and touched it before she thought. She would do a great penance for that. Her mother had talked about a picnic in a couple of weeks. Something about going out to look at the sun especially. You could do that any time. But she was wild about weenie roasts.

Very well. She would forego the pleasures of the world. She would put the picnic out of her mind and simply not pay any attention to it. She simply would not pay any attention to what her mother was saying, even though that part about smoking glass sounded funny and interesting. She wanted to ask about that, but she didn't. She would be rapt in prayer. She was. Only once on her way to the hermitage she had said "bang-bang" very softly.

It was that day, when she had arrived at the hermitage, that she found the wild thing there. She pushed her way into the lean-to, without looking, and then she heard it, right in front of her. And she saw it, coiled, as if about to leap.

It was a snake.

For a moment nothing stirred. Perhaps the snake was as scared to move as she was. Theresa thought of that, but the thought failed to attract her. She had never heard of holy hermits who had snakes for companions. The only thing she could remember was that one could lift up serpents and not be harmed. Theresa felt that she was not yet advanced enough in holiness to lift up serpents.

The fear went and came in her and, when she started to breathe, her breath was loud and irregular. Perhaps it was that which distressed the snake. All at once it unwound and slithered off through a slit in the side of the lean-to. Theresa leaned against a pole. Never again would she be quite sure that the snake had gone. Whenever she would come back after this, she would feel that the snake was still coiled in some corner of her cell.

Right now she couldn't afford to take any chances. She started out at once for Sister Gervaise, who would be sure to be at the convent helping old Mother Dolorosa peel the wax off the candles they used in the church so that the candles would be fresh-looking when the nuns used them on their own altar for Benediction.

It was that very day that Theresa was vouchsafed her vision. She had never been so close to the Blessed Sacrament before. That afternoon the Sisters had let her stay for Benediction right in their own chapel, and she was kneeling in the front pew between Mother Bernardine and Sister Drusilda whom she had always been afraid of. Out of the corner of her eye she could see Sister Emily looking oh, so holy.

And close as she was to the altar rail she could have touched Father Cooney when he turned around with the monstrance in his hand to give Benediction. It was then that she saw the vision.

It was not what Theresa, with some confidence, had expected. She had looked forward to seeing Our Lady, white-clad, blue-girdled, shining with something not so much a hue as a light. She had heard herself saying, "No. I can't tell you how she looked when she spoke to me. No. There aren't any colors in the world like that."

What she actually saw was something much less indescribable, but, she knew, even holier because it was connected with the Blessed Sacrament. She saw it as clear as anything. It was I H S written very plainly right across the sacred Host.

I H S. She knew what that meant. It was not, as Charlie thought, "I Have Suffered." It was not even what a king had seen before battle, "In This Sign." How could it be? The H would be wrong. No. It stood for the Holy Name. Sister Gervaise had told them about it.

Even after Father Cooney came down the steps to say the Divine Praises, Theresa could see the letters. She could read them clearly, although they were hazy in the incense. They were still there. Now she knew. God was telling her that He was there.

The lunette went back into the tabernacle and the nuns sang the "Holy God," not loud the way the men sang it on Holy Name Sunday but very high and very holy. When Theresa walked out of the chapel, she felt that she was trailing incense.

In the parlor, the realities of the waxed yellow floors, the hard-packed upholstered chairs with their smell of furniture polish, the rigidity of the table with the three old yearbooks on it, could not take Theresa's ecstasy from her. She resolved to yield to nobody the secret of what she had seen. Nobody.

So then Sister Gervaise said, "You look as though you'd had a vision!"

And Theresa said, "Oh, I did, Sister. I saw I H S on the Host."

The nun smiled. "That's lovely, Theresa. It's nice to be so near Our Lord, isn't it?" Sometimes, Sister Gervaise thought, it was good to have new impressions. She remembered how it had seemed to her when she had first entered the convent, and the joys she had found in its intimacies with holy things. Of course, Theresa had never before been that close to the altar where she could read the letters. She had been tucked away with the sixth-grade children, twenty pews back. It must have been quite an experience to see the design on the large Host, which Sister Gervaise had baked so often in the ornate molds she used.

Theresa was thinking: "So close to Our Lord!" For one moment she thought she might be a saint already, but she banished the temptation from her mind as she had been taught to do.

Then Sister Gervaise said a funny thing. She said, "I know how you feel, Theresa. I used to feel the same way when I saw the letters on the Host."

Sister had seen them, too! Theresa had always known that Sister Gervaise was a saint, but now she had proof. God had given them both the same vision. It bound them together in a holy unity. They would have—what did the Lives of the Saints call it?—a "pious rivalry in God."

So after that the miracle was inevitable.

"The children," Sister Gervaise had read to them, "saw the sun spinning in the heavens. The great rays of light shot up from it, whirled about it, and the multitude that had come to that far place was hushed in awe. Then the cries of the fearful people arose, echoing through the desolate valley."

The words kept running through her mind, connecting themselves with something her mother had said, but not very clearly. She was practicing recollection now, the way the book said. She "closed the ears of her mind to all worldly things."

She had difficulties, but the ascent of the spiritual mount was always arduous. Her mother would say, "Take that blank look off your face and listen to me." And Charlie proved to be a distraction and sometimes a thorn in her side. She had wished that he could be present at her miracle, though, of course, like the little boy in Portugal, he could not be expected to see everything. He skipped over his prayers sometimes, but Theresa made atonement for him and took longer and longer over the rosary, preparing for the miracle.

Every day she would go off alone, closing her mind to worldly things, sometimes fancying that she was on a pilgrimage, sometimes coming back to the idea of wandering in the desert. Only once Charlie and Joe found her and popped out of ambush at her.

"Bang-bang, you're dead."

She did not want to be dead but she died anyway until they left her alone and rode off on their pintos. They were always playing at the game of being Hopalong.

That reminded Theresa of something. After last Sunday, when her mother had met Sister Gervaise, she would look at Theresa when she came home from Mass and say, "Just who are you supposed to be today?" Her mother did not understand her. It was Theresa's great sorrow. Only Sister Gervaise understood her. Her mother thought she was playing a game. It was no game. Someday they would know. When the miracle happened. Everyone would see it.

She was thinking how it would be. She was on her way down to the new place she had found. It was a flat spot, hidden between rocks. Down below there was a private beach in a cove, and beyond that the ochre and blue of Lake Michigan. Sometimes people came to the beach, but they did not bother Theresa when she was being Simon on the pillar.

Today she was surprised to find such a number of people there. They were not going swimming. They did not act like picnickers. They just stood around as if they were waiting. Vaguely Theresa remembered her mother saying something about a picnic today. Something special about the day. But she had put it out of her mind because she was practicing perfection.

Across the lake the sun hung high, hazy, yet splendid. Almost, Theresa thought, she could look at it. She knew, of course, that she was imagining, but it was easy to see the sun dance. With her eyelids nearly shut, she could look at it. She closed her eyes and pressed her knuckles against the lids. She could see the sun dance.

"Bang-bang. You're dead." Joe Maguire and his Wild Westerners had discovered her. Even here. They never left you alone.

"Oh, go away," she said. She regretted it at once. She had committed a grave imperfection and must do penance. Stones in her shoes. But she was surprised. Usually, if she showed the gang that she did not want them, they would pester her, but now Joe only said, "Aw, go away yourself. We got more important things to look at than you. Whoop! Wha-oo!" The horsemen galloped down the cliff, swooping upon the innocent now gathered on the beach. Then they drew rein, and it seemed as if they, too, were waiting.

Theresa thought then, "What do I want to do most in the world right now?" And she answered herself, "Look at the sun. See the sun dance." So for what seemed a long time she shut her eyes hard. This was a better penance than putting stones in her shoes. She knelt bolt upright with her eyes closed. It was a sound from the people below that made her open them again. They were talking quite loudly. She could hear them up here. Even the boys had forgotten Hopalong and were watching—watching the sun.

Slowly, Theresa raised her eyes. Something had happened. A black edge had been bitten into the sun. Perceptibly it crept across the sun's face. Slowly the sun was covered up, except for a crescent, and then, rays and colors, vermilion, orange, fire-green . . .

Down below people were shouting. Spontaneously, some of them clapped their hands. Like at a show. Applauding the sun! They should be praying. Yet something had drawn Theresa up from her knees until she was standing, her arms outstretched toward the wonder of the skies, her heart beating like a wild thing, and all her silent voice crying out to God and Our Lady, "I love you!"

It was late in the afternoon when Theresa had reached the convent. All those hours she had stayed in her retreat. After the sun had come out again, with the fires leaving the heavens; after the people on the beach had gone home, the boys becoming Hopalong again; right through lunchtime and into the afternoon, Theresa had remained rooted, silent, fulfilled. She was like one in love. And for those moments, though there was no one to see her, Theresa had been beautiful.

Then she came down and walked across to the convent, just a little girl again with briar-scratched legs and bruised knees and protruding teeth, with her wind-sanded hair pulled straight back and caught up by a limp bow, with her nose slightly peeled and freckles standing out on her forehead.

She walked slowly, to music. This time she would tell Sister. Everybody had seen her miracle. She had a duty now to all the world.

She drew up short, stopped her almost processional walk. She was frightened. She did not want people coming around and asking questions. She did not want to be like Theresa Neumann or St. Bernadette.

She felt exactly the way she had felt when she found the snake in the hermitage. She was afraid.

She would give anything in the world to be with Joe and Charlie and the boys, riding down a ravine into a corral, saying: "Bang-bang. You're dead."

Never be able to do this any more. All those people down there at the cove cheering, clapping, applauding the sun. They would know. They would be after her forever. Bishops would send for her. She could hear them:

Was it you who made the sun go black?

Did you pray for the sun to dance?

Did anything like this happen to you before?

Are you humble?

Do you think you're a saint?

Who are you to tamper with the sun?

Who are you?

Who are you?

I am Theresa Doyle. I am eleven years old. I didn't mean to do a great big miracle, just a little one.

You wanted the sun to dance, Theresa.

You know you did.

It is all your fault.

All your fault.

Things will never be the same.

Never. Never. Never.

She ran to the convent then. She sat for an awfully long time in the parlor, waiting for Sister Gervaise. Far away a bell would ring. Then the swish, swish, swish of skirts. Then buzz, buzz, in a whisper. Then the swish again. And a long, convent silence. She waited so long, with the convent floor shining up at her and the furniture polish smell, that she fell into a kind of daze.

Even Sister Gervaise did not look real, but she sat so close to her that Theresa was reassured by the familiar odor of the starch of the nun's bib.

"Don't let them send me away," Theresa said. "I just want to be like all the other children."

Sister Gervaise looked at her closely. "Of course you do. But you haven't forgotten that you want to be a saint?"

"Not a great big saint. Just a little saint."

"Yes." Sister Gervaise smiled. "That's better." She reached into her sleeve and held out her handkerchief. "Now blow your nose and tell me what this is all about."

So Theresa told her, and Sister Gervaise did not laugh. Only once she said, "Oh!" and that was when Theresa mentioned the vision of the I H S. But she didn't say anything else even when she heard about how Theresa had expected the sun to dance, but had not realized that all those people would be there to watch her miracle and that even the boys would keep still.

When she got through, Sister Gervaise said, "All right, Theresa. I see it all now."

For a moment she was silent. What should she tell this child? That her miracle was no miracle, her vision no vision? Yes. Somehow. There were great wonders in the world today, but side by side with them were the false apparitions, the pitiful delusions. Yes. She must say it.

"It was not a miracle, Theresa. It was not a vision of I H S on the host."

"But I saw it, Sister."

"So does everyone else. It was there. Like the eclipse today. It was real."

"Wasn't it anything—God gave me? Wasn't it anything special?"

"Yes, dear, it was special. The people on the shore clapped their hands for the sun, as if it were a show; but one little girl raised her heart to God."

Theresa had had a doubt left. She said, "But then—it wasn't God just talking to me alone?"

"In a way it was. God puts wonderful things in the world but only one little girl saw Him in His wonders today. The rest looked through smoked glasses. You saw it."

"Yes, Sister." Her voice had the tone of classroom acquiescence.

"You must always see God in everything."

"Everything? All kinds of things?"

"Absolutely everything."

Theresa looked at Sister Gervaise. The room, the world, came back into focus. When she spoke, her voice had its old ring.

"Even in Hopalong Cassidy?"

And it was Sister Gervaise's reply that had sealed her adoration then and for all the years to come, for Sister Gervaise had said, "Yes, dear. Perhaps *especially* in Hopalong Cassidy."

"Oh, bother," Mother Bernardine was saying to herself. She had put the lights out in the kitchen after she had got Lady, the dog, a drink. It was twenty-five minutes before eleven. There, shining down across the snow of the clothes yard, was a light. It could come from nowhere but Gervaise's window.

There was really no excuse for this. Other nights, when the play had been in preparation, she could overlook it. But Gervaise didn't have that much to do now. And it wasn't very grateful of her either, when just that night she had practically gone against her principles to say yes to a banquet for the students, when what she really thought was that they should be trained to acts of charity without visible awards.

Reverend Mother went upstairs purposively. She hoped, too, after the good talking-to she had given Rosemary Morrison, that Sister Gervaise would keep her eye on that girl a little bit more. The very idea of going around "steady" with a boy. What was Gervaise thinking of, to allow it? And if Mrs. Morrison knew about it—well, you could imagine. Although Rosemary tried to let on that she did. Even that she approved. Ridiculous. Mother Bernardine knew Mrs. Morrison better than that. She was a fine woman.

Sure enough. The light was coming from beneath Sister Gervaise's door. Without pausing Mother Bernardine rapped smartly, then opened the door. Sister Gervaise seemed to jump, startled. She was still at her desk.

"Please, Sister," Mother Bernardine said, "I have asked you before. You need your rest."

She did not wait for a reply, closing the door again.

Sister Gervaise looked at her silver watch. Twenty of eleven! Oh no! And this had been the night when she could have gone to bed. She shouldn't have leaned her head against that wall. Not for a minute.

Just for a minute.

Chapter 6

WELL, she probably would have done it herself.

There was no need for Father Cooney to make such a fuss over it anyway. But, then, he wouldn't if she hadn't gone after him about the singing at the nine-o'clock Mass. And she wouldn't have said a word about that if Sister Consolata hadn't told her that very morning that the pastor had already asked her to take over the children's singing, as if Consolata didn't have enough already with her art classes.

Sometimes Sister Gervaise could not understand Father Cooney. If he had already approached Sister Consolata about the music, why had he spoken to her about it yesterday? It had come up just after he had asked her to take the St. Patrick's Day play, and she had demurred because she was so busy. Then he had broached that music thing. Just every now and then she thought that the pastor had a strange sense of humor.

But there was no joke about what they had said this morning. When Sister Consolata told her that she had been drafted to take over the children's choir she had promised to go to Father Cooney and lay the law down about what kind of hymns would be sung.

"But you can't just tell the pastor, can you?" Sister Consolata had asked.

"Yes. Doesn't the Pope want the right kind of music? And isn't the Bishop doing his best to get it?"

"Yes, but . . ."

"If a higher superior commands something it is the duty of the inferior to enforce it. That's right in the Rule." She laughed. "I feel like Sister Emily."

Armed with the Holy Rule she went forth to do battle with Father Cooney in the cause of Sister Consolata and the *motu proprio* of Pius X. The only difficulty was that the pastor anticipated her and bore down on her, his usual smile of greeting at half mast.

"I understand that you have asked Sister Consolata to take over the choir. She will if she can have the proper hymns."

The pastor interrupted her. "What kind of way is that to stack chairs?" he called.

"What way?" How did she know how they were stacked? She hadn't turned the lights up again in the auditorium. She could trust Mrs. Doyle.

"Right plank up against the stage. How do you expect us to get the head table there for the CYO supper?"

It was incredible that . . . If you wanted something done right you had to . . . What could she say?

Father Cooney sighed and shook his head. His chin settled into the folds of his neck. "If you want something done right you have to do it yourself," he said. "Now I've got to get those blackguards of boys to take all those chairs out of there. We never had this trouble when we ran the parish shows. The men always did up the chairs after, and we had a nice dance for ourselves, too."

"I know. Mr. MacGill told me."

"He was right. Well—wasn't he?"

"Yes. I . . . I think he was."

"So now I'm telling you—I'm not asking you, mind you—you'll have a dance after the St. Patrick's show, and I'll see to the way the chairs are stacked myself."

Who said there was going to be a St. Patrick's show?

"Look, Father," she said, "if there's going to be a St. Patrick's night, then the young people can do it themselves. They won't need me. They can put on any old thing they want."

"Oh, they can, can they? Not while I'm around here, they can't. There'll be supervision of things in this parish while the Bishop keeps me here. And that's what you're supposed to be doing."

"I'm supposed to put on the high-school plays."

Their voices were too loud. People coming out of Mass were looking at them. And, with a gasp, Sister Gervaise realized that Mrs. Morrison had just passed them, had bowed to them, and had had, in return for her civility, a very cold nod indeed. What would she think now? And after that gray-dress business, too! Should she run after her, tell her she had just been abstracted? But she couldn't. The pastor was still talking.

". . . and you with a vow of obedience, I hear."

"All right, Father," she replied. "I'm sure it'll all be very nice, and I am very sorry about the chairs, but as far as obedience goes, that's just what I came to talk to you about."

"You did, did you?"

"I did, Father. It's about this church music. I told Sister Consolata I would speak to you. You see, if she has the children's choir, they've got to sing the right things."

"Of course they do. Don't they?"

"Well, they don't now. That's sure."

"They sing better than the big choir. At least the kids

don't stop me when I'm getting to the Consecration. Now you take that Gregorian. You have her teach them that."

"Why, I didn't know . . ."

"There's a lot of things you don't know about me. Tell her to teach them a Gregorian Mass—that Mass of the Angels, for instance. That's a nice short one. But no Credo."

"You like Gregorian because it's short?"

"There's worse reasons. If you've got to get the people in and out of church, there's things you have to think about if the next crowd's going to come in. That young fellow there of mine—he preaches too long."

He did. But at least Father Rolfe was interesting and he had a nice voice. This was getting nowhere. "I'll tell Sister Consolata you said to go ahead, then."

"You'll tell her no such thing. Just what I said. She can have them learn that Mass, but we're not going to throw out all the good old hymns that the kids get a lot of devotion out of. No, sir! Only tell her to pep them up a little bit. They sing 'em too slow."

"Indeed they do. And if you pep them up, they'll all sound like what they are—fox trots."

"Fox trots, is it?" he laughed. "Well, that's better than bo-peep or whatever it is the kids do nowadays, anyway." He looked grave, and shook his head almost sadly. "And you know what I hear?"

"No, Father. I don't."

"I hear the Bishop, God bless us, is going to forbid the wedding march. Would you believe it?"

"Oh, I hope so!"

"God forgive you," he said; "you've never been married."

There was no answering that. She said nothing, and Father

72 ☞

Cooney went on. "It's no wonder, with all the changes they're making, the old people think they've left the Church." He started to turn away, and then looked back. "Tell your Consolata I'll take care of my end of the church and she can take care of hers, whatever business it is of yours. And as for you—let me have a nice minstrel show for St. Pat's."

Sister Gervaise watched him retreating up the steps of the church. She wondered. Could it be that he was taking her for a ride? No. She couldn't believe it. And as for that musical show, she would have strictly nothing to do with it. Nothing. The young people could put it on without her. Oh yes, she would supervise it, see that nothing out of the way was in it, but that was absolutely all.

She would concentrate on *Murder in the Cathedral*. There was enough to do to make that come out right. It was a beautiful thing. That was her duty: to make beautiful things. It wasn't right to compromise. If *they* wanted to put on a cheap old vaudeville, they couldn't hold her responsible. Besides, March was only a month away, and there just wasn't time to fuss with inconsequential things. She would wash her hands of it.

And for quite a long time that is precisely what she did.

February, she knew, was always a bad month, but this February was the worst of all. The midyear examinations were over and the students had no incentive. The nuns had nothing to look forward to except Lent. Sister Inez, the Spanish Sister, startled the community one evening at recreation by saying, "Zees is hell."

Even Mother Dolorosa looked up from her embroidery.

~ 73

Nothing ever amazed her into idleness, but she paused for a moment now, and then settled back, sure that at last her hearing was playing tricks on her.

"Why, Sister," Sister Roseanne, who was still a novice and somewhat untamed, cried, "you shock me. And when you can shock me, that's something!" She laughed at herself, but her laugh trickled off as she caught Sister Emily's eye.

"What I say? Eet ees so. Yes. I tell that to, what you call them, the *cabritos,* and I say, see, cheeldren. Now you know what is hell!"

Mother Bernardine was amused, but it was obvious, as she stroked Lady, that she was wondering just what was going on in Sister Inez's classroom. Really there was only one thing wrong with Sister Inez, and that was that she did not like dogs. Aside from that she was all right.

"Why do you say that, Sister?" the Superior asked.

"I say to them: Think back—it was Christmas. Think forward—it is Easter. Between, in this North, is what? An eenfeenite distance forward. That is hell. And you—you can go to hell."

It was Sister Drusilda who was most amused. That kind of thing tickled her. Her mouth turned down in a smile. Why, she had even thought Father Cooney's constant gibing at Dolorosa and Consolata, that improbable combination of names, was amusing until at last it had worn so very thin.

"That's good," she said. "I'll have to remember to use it."

It was, Sister Gervaise thought, an infinite distance back all right, but scarcely an infinite distance forward. The days were running away from her, speeding toward the time for the spring play which needed to go into rehearsal soon, and she couldn't get the students to do anything except talk about this extravaganza of theirs.

Everything seemed to be marking time. Margaret Fleming's Jim had come back from service the other day, and, as far as was known, things were going smoothly enough. At least one could presume so, because Margaret had not come over to the convent. That was the trouble with being a nun: you got interested in something and then for a long while you didn't hear any more about it. Sometimes you never heard. So many continued stories of which you could not get the next month's issue.

Then, of course, there were the things you expected to happen which never took form. Mrs. Morrison had never mentioned the gray chiffon dress; Mother Bernardine had not again referred to late lights; Sister Consolata was training the children beautifully in the better hymns, without a murmur from Father Cooney.

Somebody had been talking to her. She mustn't go wool-gathering like this at recreation. Sister Consolata wanted to play charades. They had not played charades for a long time, for recently they had been playing twenty questions. Before that it had been that spelling game, ghosts. Anyway, they always had a good time at St. Rita's during recreation, that was one thing about it here. They weren't like those college nuns at Marycliff, too important to have a good time. St. Rita's was a pleasant community.

They played charades.

It must have been the day after that, she thought later, that she had first noticed something wrong with Rosemary, although it was not until Shrove Tuesday, Mardi Gras, that anything serious developed. That second episode she would always remember, because it was the day after the dramatic banquet.

But the first time she had noticed had been earlier. Late February. She knew that she had been surprised, because if anyone ought to be downcast it was Theresa. She had been working hard to make Joe Maguire so much as look at her. Lately she had taken to pulling her lip down over her upper teeth, so that it made her look like the older members of the British royal family. But what could the poor thing do with such competition? There was no doubt about it, Rosemary was a little beauty.

So it was not lack of success in matters of the heart that was troubling Rosemary. Something else. And Sister Gervaise was sure that her cheeks were tear-stained when she found her alone in the cloakroom that dim afternoon.

"What's the matter, dear?" Sister Gervaise had asked.

Rosemary was furious at being discovered. She was not accepting sympathy from anyone. "Nothing," she had said. "There is nothing the matter with me." And she had brushed off Sister Gervaise's outstretched hand and gone down the corridor, out the door, to where her mother was waiting for her in the car.

But there was something, Ash Wednesday, that she could not deny.

Oh yes. They had had the banquet. Nick Collasanto had assured her that it was tops. Father Cooney had been at it and Father Rolfe had made a real funny speech and the food was swell. By dint of careful inquiry she discovered that Joe had taken Rosemary home afterward, so that was that. And the orchestra was cool, the cats were cool, in fact the whole evening, she discovered, was cool.

She was glad it had been cool.

When would she ever get over that feeling? Wasn't it silly? She didn't particularly want to be there, she probably wouldn't have enjoyed herself at all; yet when the music had drifted over to her cell and her imagination had been filled with all her children gathered together in the auditorium at the party that she had worked so hard to get for them, she had for just one minute wondered if they thought about her at all. If they thought about her sitting here alone, foolishly, with her lights out, looking across the snow-covered playground at the empty niche.

Ridiculous. The next day it had meant nothing at all even when she had heard that Father Cooney had made a rather nice speech about her. Though of course she was glad he had been tactful enough to do that, no matter what he really thought.

She had met with a rather listless class which at last she had galvanized into some semblance of activity, mainly by board drill which she hated, and rapid-fire questioning which she loved. Toward the end of the fifty minutes they were beginning to show some signs of humanity. All except Rosemary.

Classes such as that really taxed you. Sister Gervaise was rather limp as she sat at her consultation desk, prefecting the late-punishment session. Yet, from what she had heard of other schools, St. Rita's was a paradise. She had never really had a disciplinary problem, she thought, and it must be awful for a teacher who had. In fact, unless you preferred teaching to any other job in the world, it must be awful enough anyway. But for herself, she saw it as a constant challenge, thirty-five against one, and she remembered with gratitude something Mother Dolorosa had said to her years ago, when she was new in the classroom.

She had been complaining that year about the few really good students who came to her, and Mother Dolorosa had said, "Anybody can teach good students, Sister. It takes a *teacher* to save the bad ones."

Save the bad ones. She tackled the themes before her, the bad ones, attempting to analyze the causes of the deficiencies of each. Mostly, her mind confirmed, the cause was lack of self-discipline. It wasn't that they didn't know; they simply didn't bother. The minutes extra, one more reading of the homework paper and Johnny could spell all right. It wasn't true that they hadn't been taught spelling; it was true that they had not been taught discipline, care, order, the duty of revision, and they seemed to hate accuracy as they did hell's pains. Now take this . . .

She looked up to discover Rosemary standing in front of her.

"I'm sorry. I didn't hear you. I was doing other things."

Rosemary did not smile. "Sister Consolata sent me. She told me to see you."

"Sit down."

Rosemary sat gracefully. She said nothing.

"Well? Here I am. Here you are. What's it all about?"

"I don't think you'll agree with me. Nobody does."

"Perhaps not. Tell me so that I can disagree, then."

"I want to change schools."

"You what?" Here it was, the second semester well under way, and Rosemary in her senior year. "It's a little late," Sister Gervaise went on quietly. "But of course we'll have to see if it can be arranged."

Rosemary reacted with a start of incredulity. All students did. They were so pitifully lacking in defenses.

"You mean, you think I should?"

"Certainly. No student should be obliged to stay at St.

Rita's. Not if she doesn't want to. And lately I haven't thought you were very happy. Where were you thinking of going?"

"Any place. Some boarding school."

"I see. Now I wonder what boarding school would accept students at this time of year?"

"I don't know. Sister Consolata didn't know either. She didn't want me to go but she said to come around and see you anyway. So I came."

"You mean you didn't really want to talk about it with me, but Sister Consolata insisted?"

Rosemary's politeness struggled with her honesty. Finally honesty won, and she said, "Yes, Sister."

"Then don't you talk to me, Rosemary. It isn't everybody you can talk to. But now that I know this much, I'll see what can be done for you. If anything. Maybe there is some school that would take in an A student for the last few months. I know you have a good reason. Don't you?"

"Yes, Sister."

"You see a girl doesn't run out on things when everything *looks* as if it's all right with her, unless it's something serious." She did not look at Rosemary, her eyes fastened to her hands, her fingertips picking up specks on the desk. "You know what you're giving up." She did not say the word, Joe, but they both understood. "And next year I suppose you'll be going to college, and you'll be away anyway, but if these few months are that important to you—well, they're that important, and that's all there is to it. I suppose you'll be going to Marycliff?"

"No, Sister."

"No? I thought you were signed up for it."

"My mother wants me to go East to college. She wants me to go to Poughkeepsie."

"She does!" It was always a blow when the parents of a girl chose a non-Catholic school for her. It was even a blow, Sister Gervaise acknowledged to herself, when they chose another Catholic college over the Cliffs, as if the parents had not been satisfied with the teaching at St. Rita's. But that a pillar of the parish, like Mrs. Morrison, should even dream of sending Rosemary elsewhere—East, of all places— that was too much.

"She says she wants me to be fully rounded."

"I'm sure. And what do you want?"

"I want to go to the Cliffs."

"You will. I'll help you go any place you want for the rest of this year, if you think it over for a few days and come around again. But if you want to go to the Cliffs, that's where you're going. I'll see your mother. Believe me, I'll see her." A thought struck her then. "What about your father? What does he want?" What about that man who must, all six feet of him, be lurking somewhere in the background?

"Dad? He'd like for me to go to the Cliffs."

"I see. Then it's the Cliffs for you, young Rosemary."

An auto horn honked from outside. Rosemary rose abruptly.

"That's my mother." She grasped her books and papers, and, as she did so, remembered something. "I almost forgot." She took a pink-tinted letter from one of her books and handed it to the nun. "It's for a spiritual bouquet. Mother would like Sister Consolata to make up a nice one for something special. It's just to read: 'For Monsignor.' Is ten dollars enough?"

"Certainly. Thank your mother for it."

The envelope was not addressed to Sister Consolata. In a florid script it bore the name of Mother Bernardine. For a flash Sister Gervaise again disapproved of Mrs. Morrison. It was as blatant as if the envelope had been addressed: Ten Dollars. Attention: Mother Superior! But Consolata was to do the work.

"Monsignor"—Sister Gervaise wondered who that could be. What monsignor did Mrs. Morrison know? Really, it was none of her business.

She said good-by to Rosemary and watched her hurry off.

Supper was over before she found an opportunity to talk to Sister Consolata since the entire afternoon had been spent in getting the church ready for Ash Wednesday.

"What was that all about?" Sister Gervaise asked. "And why send Rosemary to me?"

"She wanted to talk to you."

"She said she didn't."

"I know. But I could see through her. She's just afraid of you. They're all afraid of you."

That isn't true! Many aren't. Well, Theresa isn't. And why should they be afraid of her? She certainly didn't intend to terrorize them. Or was that really why she had no disciplinary problems? Maybe they were afraid.

"That's funny. I'm not a bit afraid of myself. I just feel all benignant inside. Anyway, that isn't the point. What's the matter with Rosemary?"

Sister Consolata fumbled for a moment. "I shouldn't really tell you."

"Wild horses wouldn't drag it out of you?"

"No. But . . ."

"But?"

Sister Consolata's fresh and unlined face became aged with anxiety and disapproval. "Rosemary told me," she said, "that she hated her mother!"

Chapter 7

IT WAS NOT until March 13 that Sister Gervaise saw the rehearsal of what she always called the extravaganza, and then she went strictly as a censor. She had cause to be glad later.

Everybody was in it, including Rosemary, who had not so much as mentioned her pre-lenten turmoil. Even her father was in it. He was not at all what Sister Gervaise had imagined he would be—a big, soft-spoken, henpecked man. On the contrary, as she watched him among the groups made up of half the parish, he seemed to be the life of the party. In the show he was the master of ceremonies, if you could call it that, and he was surprisingly good, although the production itself was endless and formless.

The parishioners urged Sister Gervaise throughout the evening to do some directing, but she would not. Sitting alone, a smile of amusement painted on her face so that she would not appear to be disapproving, she sturdily held to her guns. This was not her play. She was there merely because the pastor had ordered the show to be supervised. That was that.

She watched the numbers unroll, amused by some, bored by others. The production had no head or tail to it.

Then something happened. Margaret Fleming and Jimmy

Dugan had just sung, rather significantly, she thought, "Getting to know you, getting to like you." Then a little boy came out on the stage. There was a chorus behind him, but it was insignificant. The boy was about eleven, chosen from the grade school, she supposed. He was neatly, too neatly, dressed, his hair slicked down with something resembling axle grease. As yet, he had no face to speak of, just eyes. But then he sang.

His soprano voice had a coloratura quality, but, rare in any coloratura, his lower register was warm and tremendously moving. Although he stood stock-still in the middle of the stage there was in him an animal desire to move that no amount of bad instruction could suppress.

When he had finished, and before the chorus could ruin the effect, quite against her will Sister Gervaise applauded.

Then the entire cast took it up, and Sister Gervaise was on her feet, hastening toward the stage. She could not have this ruined! Oh dear, dear, she thought, there was so much talent here! Visions of bits of the other acts came back to her. Yes. They could be good. Even Margaret. Yes, she could do something with Margaret. . . .

"I don't want to interfere . . ." she began.

There was a chorus of voices: "Oh, you're not! Come on, be a sport, Sister!"

Mr. Morrison jumped down from the stage. Although he was perfectly respectful, his voice made her feel as if he had clapped her on the back. "O.K., Sister! It's all yours!"

"Oh no! I just thought I'd make some suggestions."

"Go ahead! Suggest away!"

"Then what's this—extravaganza—all about?"

"About? Why—it's a revue, I guess."

"Fine. How does it hang together?"

Nick Collasanto, she thought it was, yelled down, "You tell us!" And they all laughed and applauded.

Afraid of her? Who was afraid of her? Sister Consolata had been wrong.

"All right. All right. Bring me the script. Cast, get off that stage for twenty minutes. Then be back. All of you."

She took what there was of a script. That other something that happened to her once in a while was happening. It was like a wave of self-confidence, like the feeling that a musical maestro must have with the score before him and an obedient orchestra ready. She could not fail. She had this group in the hollow of her hands.

How often, since she had entered the convent, had she tried to beat down this feeling? It would not be defeated. It was a violation of humility, she knew, but what could she do about it? There were some people just born that way. In the old days, if she just walked on a stage . . . Now, if she just walked into a classroom . . .

And she had tried so hard. No matter how quiet she would be at the beginning of recreation, somebody always got her to start the charades. By the end of a party, even as a young girl, she had taken over. Hadn't intended to . . . did nothing about it. But it always just happened. Why?

Her mind raced along through the script, the dragged-in dances, the unmotivated songs. The cast: Doyle, Collasanto, Blaumberg, Flores, Ziglatsky, Du Bois.

"All the world is Irish—all the world is Irish today!"

There was a tune to fit that. Yes, there was.

Margaret Fleming, an Irish colleen, surrounded by little foreign children? Chinese? Japanese? Singing, "Getting to know you?" Then on comes a Spaniard—no, too ordinary—

a—well, why not an Oriental of some kind? Yes. Jimmy Dugan had been in Korea. He would know.

Then that little boy. He was a Polish type. Good. A refugee wandering from country to country—and at last the warm heart of Ireland takes him in. He becomes *Irish*.

"I've got it!" she cried.

The players came hastening back.

"Look! Here's the idea. This is St. Patrick's Day. You've got to think of this all the time. You see, St. Patrick is different. It's a national feast, yes. But it's not like any other national feast in the world, because Patrick was a saint. That lets him belong to all of us, lets all be Irish for one day, because he does belong to all of us, too, don't you see?

"And the Irish. They're spread all over the world. They're not just a nation—they're a Cause. And everywhere they've gone, they've brought something beautiful and wonderful and warm. And holy. Maybe they've been robbed of their heritage of learning, but God made them to be the school-masters and scholars of the world, and they still are. They teach what they know. What you couldn't starve out of them. The Faith!

"So tonight it isn't just a—an—extravaganza you're putting on. It's a bright, beautiful, happy communion of the living saints. It's Catholic. Because it is Irish."

They did not applaud when she had finished. The silence was a better tribute. More quietly she went on and outlined her new plot, weaving things together with a significance they all felt.

"Now don't let that meaning spoil the fun of it," she counseled. "Just keep it way down at the bottom of your minds, and it'll come out. Don't worry about it."

So she started at the beginning, motivating each scene for

them. When she got to the Margaret and Jim scene, she changed it all around. It was a good place to introduce the children's dances and songs. Then, because Margaret had a small, sweet voice, she had the children grow quieter and quieter, until it almost seemed that Margaret emerged from among them, and her singing had the quality of a lullaby. Then the oriental prince appeared, and Sister Gervaise took liberties with the words. "Getting to know you, getting to love you . . ."

She stopped them in the middle of their duet, going up on the stage, whispering to the girl.

"Margaret," she said, "what are you saying?"

Baffled, the girl repeated the words mechanically.

"Now look at Jimmy. Remember what you told me before he came home. Do you?"

"Oh yes."

"Are you quite sure yet?"

"No, Sister."

"But you want it to turn out right, don't you?"

"So much."

"Now just say the words again. Look at him. Mean them. Just say them."

Margaret said them. The next time she sang them, that "something" had happened. They weren't words any more. They were an expression of what was in her heart.

"Getting to know you, getting to love you . . ."

Yes. The listeners felt it. It was good. And Jimmy picked up the feeling when his big basso came in like an orchestra under Margaret's fluting.

When the break came after that scene, Jimmy called down, "I didn't know nuns went to shows!"

"We don't," Sister Gervaise answered.

"Then how did you know?"

"Know what?"

"How this scene went in the original? The kids and all. You must have seen it. It's almost the same way."

"I—I didn't . . ."

"Oh, come on now, Sister. You've been sneaking out nights!"

"Maybe that's it," she answered in the same vein. She didn't say any more. How did she know? She had read the song. If a song were any good at all, it would set a situation. If you really knew your business, you could make the situation come to life again. That's all she had done. But if she said that to them, they would all be impressed.

They would think it was genius or some nonsense, while it was really an experience. So she said nothing, letting them think that in some way she was acquainted with the play from which this music came. What was the play? She didn't even know that. She said nothing and she felt better for it. It was an act of humility to offset the wave of pride she had had before. She hoped God would take note of it. She felt He would.

After she had directed the little boy through several scenes (Stanley, his name was—ridiculous, Stanislaus, of course), Mr. Morrison came up beside her in the darkness.

"Pretty good, isn't he?"

"He's wonderful." She had released him, letting him do pretty much what he wanted to do, motivating the others around him. He had, she knew, that strange magnetism that no mere talent could compensate for. A great future. The others on stage became mere scenery. If only one, just one, of her own drama students had that quality. Well, you couldn't expect everything. Rosemary was beautiful and

Theresa had gifts for characterization. Nick had fire, and Joe was six feet tall.

"Sure is," agreed Mr. Morrison. "It's too bad, isn't it?"

"What is?"

"That kid. He's got only a year to live."

"Oh no!" Her voice was louder than it should have been. The cast looked up, startled, but she waved them on.

"Yep. Sugar diabetes. Kids don't survive it very often."

Now she was glad that she had taken this task on herself. If only for one night, she could bring this radiant talent to a little world! What kind of values were those? They were the values of her father's milieu not of hers. Yet, wasn't there some truth in them?

The next set she had motivated with a harmless and aimed malice. Joe Maguire, an Irish boy, was torn between Miss France (Theresa) and Miss Southern Belle (Rosemary). A French girl needed chic and vivacity, both of which Theresa had. It would give Theresa a chance, which she certainly was taking. Just for the fun of it, Sister Gervaise would let Theresa win—on the stage. But it also would give Rosemary a chance to look pretty and that would satisfy her.

Then came the riposte. They had wound the song "All the World Is Irish Today" through the entire show. Mr. Morrison had been developed into a guide for a world tour of the Irish in all climes, and it was his brilliance that capped the climax, with a final phrase:

"And all the world's named Cooney, named Cooney,
And all the world's named Cooney,
He's the Father of us all!"

Not terribly clever, but the pastor would be charmed. No harm.

89

At last Sister Gervaise gave her little curtain talk, thanking them, telling them to be there promptly at seven tomorrow, and reminding them that they had a terrific job to do if they were to round this thing off into any kind of shape in only three days. She warned them to follow Mr. Morrison with deathlike devotion, wondering secretly how he would ever master all the cues so as to lead them. Then Mr. Morrison whispered to her, "Where's your father now?"

Before she had a chance to think of something evasive she had whispered back, "Finishing a run in St. Louis." And then she was really embarrassed at the things Mr. Morrison said about her, although it was all done jocosely, in a kind of midway-at-the-carnival fashion.

"Ladies and gentlemen," he bellowed, "you have all seen and heard this wonderful little lady—this amazing little Irish colleen—put life and blood and the spirit of Old Erin into our supercolossal and magnificent opus! Nobody but an Irish girl could do it! You've watched the professional touch, the real show-biz McCoy! You've seen in action the daughter of the great Michael Rhodes"—her father's name was Richard, but that didn't matter—"now finishing up a grand coast-to-coast personal appearance on the shores of the Mississippi in St. Louis! I know that it goes without saying that when this little lady cracks the whip, we dance! Her word is law. What she says goes. Are you with me—for the Hollywood and Broadway nun—Sister Gervaise!"

They roared their approval.

Back in the convent, Mother Bernardine did not roar, but she did approve.

"I'm glad you thought better of it, Sister. I didn't want to interfere, but I do think we should not refuse any reasonable request of the pastor."

She said it with a good deal of personal feeling because she still had not got around to refusing the Bishop on that summer-school business. Soon she would have to.

The rehearsals the next two nights were a joy. She had never had better attention or more perfect obedience, and, somewhat like the proverbial green bay tree, the talent bloomed. There was something else, though, she knew, beyond her own drive that made them anxious to do their best. Something was in the air, some expectancy possessed them. Her only worry was the impossible task set for Mr. Morrison, to cue entrances and exits through a whole evening, and pretty involved ones at that. Inevitably, she mourned, these would be ragged, but without any time, what could you do? The best will in the world couldn't overcome that handicap, and however nicely the show went, bad timing could ruin it. That would be too bad because—she hated to admit it—the thing was good.

Yet the miracle did happen.

From her perch in the balcony where she could see and still be out of the way, she had observed how a hall could really fill up. She had been gratified by the attendance at her own plays, but if the fire-law people didn't say anything about this mob scene, Mother Bernardine need have no worries about future entertainments. At the door, too, they were all buying chances on the raffle to be held immediately afterward. This would be a big money-maker all right.

Mrs. Morrison, she saw, had come down the center aisle and taken the seat next to where the clergy would sit. It was her right, she supposed, as president of the Altar and Rosary Society—and several other things. She was almost formally dressed and was wearing a large and annoying hat that Sister Gervaise hoped she would remove.

Mrs. Doyle, she knew, was backstage, helping out with the costumes.

Costumes! I wonder if . . .

Suddenly she leaped up and flew down the gallery stairs. If only this mob, this gang at the door, would let her through. Oh, stop being friendly, she prayed, just let me get downstairs to classroom 3-A. Yes, I'm very well. It's nice to see you, too. Pardon. Excuse me. Oh, how are you, Mrs. Collins? Yes. She's doing fine. Pardon. Sorry. Please—I must get through!

There was a bit of air on the lower stairs and she breathed it in deeply. Let there be time!

At the boys' dressing room she called, "Stanislaus!" but there was no response. Stanley succeeded better.

It was as bad as she had feared. His mother had dressed her little boy for the stage so that he would look nice. And Stanley wasn't that kind of boy at all. He shouldn't have his hair slicked back, his tie caught with a pin, the creases in his trousers perfect. Poor boy, he didn't even look human.

"Stand there," she ordered. "Don't budge an inch!"

Up the iron stairs. People backstage knew her and made themselves thin against the wall. She ran out on the stage and looked out through the center curtains, a thing she had always forbidden everybody else to do.

"Look out, Sister!"

Something fell behind her, narrowly missing her. That was unusual. But what were those men on the two ladders doing? Stretching something just inside the proscenium. Not lights. She'd attended to that herself. Oh, bother. It didn't matter.

The clergy seats were still empty. In a way, that was good. But she had to find Father Rolfe. There. She spotted him over in a corner talking with Mr. Collasanto. Get him! She thought of asking Nick to go out, but she had tried sending him on an errand once. Never again!

She went herself. As she emerged from the stage door there was a little flurry of applause from the group nearest, but, thank God, it died, and she got through to Father Rolfe.

"Father," she asked, "have you got an old pair of pants?"

The assistant looked down at his legs. "Fairly old," he said.

Oh, don't do that to me! "I mean really old. In your room—that we could tear up? And an old shirt?"

"My room's torn up already."

"Listen. Can you dash over and bring me back one old pair of pants and a shirt—even Father Cooney's?"

Now he saw that she was desperate. "Sure, Sister."

"Quick. Bring them up the iron stairs as fast as you can."

"You bet."

He's a good lad—I mean, a fine priest, she thought gratefully. And, although the opening chorus had started without Stanley before the priest had returned, it was still all right, as the boy did not have to come on until later.

Stanislaus was exactly where she had left him, only somebody had done a still more ghastly thing to him. He had been made up. Oh no! He looked like a pretty little girl. Stanley just wasn't that kind of boy.

"Look, Stan. Go in that dressing room and wash that slop off your face. Then"—she pulled a scissors out of her pocket and began ripping at Father Rolfe's trousers, cutting off all the lower parts, tearing both legs into jagged rags, making an equal horror of the shirt—"put these on."

"These?"

"Yes."

"Do I hafta?"

"Yes."

He went in and after a few moments called her. Upstairs, they were already at the "All the World Is Ireland" song. Hurry.

The dressing room, of course, was deserted except for themselves.

Stanley looked better. She rumpled up his hair and he looked better still.

"There," she said at last.

There was an odd expression in the boy's eyes.

"Do I have to wear these?"

"You do."

He was silent a moment. "Can't I wear my own clothes?" He looked down at his pink legs. Poor kid. He was embarrassed.

"Wait a minute," she said. "I'm not through yet."

She took a black make-up stick and for good measure put a daub on his face.

"Now rub some of this on your legs."

He did. He smiled. He felt fully clothed.

"Now go up on that stage and be wonderful!"

She ran through the corridor and walked more sedately up the back stairs. People were still coming, but in trickles now, so that she could elude them. One thing she wanted to see was Stanley's entrance. Then in her gallery, where no one ever came, she knew she was safe. The clergy, their backs black against the lights, were all in place. There was one vacant seat, though, next to Mrs. Morrison. On the stage things, for the moment anyway, were going smoothly. She was in time.

Why was she angry? Up here, away from everyone, why did she always feel like this? There was nothing to make her angry. Yet every time a play was in progress, she felt the same way—just as if she were angry. Oh no, she wasn't nervous. Not in the least bit.

She wished they wouldn't let the latecomers in during a scene. That back door squeaked. It banged sometimes. She expected it to bang, but it didn't. Rosemary! Rosemary! Get into the light! How often have I told you . . . Oh, you idiots down there, stop falling over chairs in the dark! Next thing you know, somebody's going to say afterward he couldn't hear the actors. How could they hear with a herd of elephants milling around?

A man walked all the way down front. Ought to know better. Oh, he was sitting in the vacant seat next to the clergy. Probably a priest. Even a priest ought to know better. The man's back looked familiar.

Theresa was doing all right. Why, she actually looked pretty. No. Attractive. More attractive than Rosemary. Not prettier.

Close that door downstairs. You're letting light in!

This wasn't possible. Her own door, the door to the gallery was opening. Nobody was allowed up here. Must be some strangers—and just before Stanley's entrance. She must evict them, though.

No strangers. It was Jeanne Collins. How dare she! She knew better.

"Jeanne! Go down where you belong." Careful of your whisper. It carries.

"Sister, where are you?" Jeanne was blinded, coming from

the light into the dark gallery. She was bumping into things.

"Here I am. Unless it's life or death . . ."

"It's just this."

In the darkness a folder was forced into her hands. Then Jeanne Collins beat a hasty and strategic retreat. Not even a message. How utterly ridiculous. Oh! It was the program. Why now? Why up here? She turned her attention to the stage just in time. The children were beginning their various national dances. Now watch. Now . . . now . . .

Now, from far downstage right, appeared a ragged little boy, alone down there. Deliberately she had tipped the stage for him, putting all the others upstage and left. The children! Those wonderful children!

They weren't acting at all. The last time they had seen Stanley he had been a Fauntleroy, and now look at him! Those glorious children started to laugh.

Stanley stopped. He looked down at himself, and for an awful moment she thought he was going to cry. But Stanley wasn't being Stanley—he was lost in this other world. His head came up, proud, defiant, and that magnificent voice swept over the auditorium. Then the children went back into doing what they were supposed to do, mechanically, according to their training, but no falsity could matter now. The effect had been made, and there was no falsity in the ragged little boy who went from group to group of strange, beautifully garbed youngsters, who, as he approached, retreated from him. And all the pathos of the young and lost was in his singing.

Pathos? The audience could not know what she knew—that this was a dying boy. But all boys were dying. There was no one who could not feel that inevitable imminence of tragedy that is in a young boy singing. The voice so soon to be lost. The great art almost immediately to perish. One day soon the silver sound to crack like a broken bell.

She was glad when the waves of applause demanded an encore. During the repetition she could listen and not be swept away by her own thinking. Also, during the applause, she had had a chance to blow her nose.

The intermission came then, leaving with the audience, as she had intended, the memory of this boy. Just before the lights went up she retreated into her more remote hide-out, the light booth. She could not see the audience from there, but she could feel them. Warm. Delighted. A bit sentimental —ah well, all right.

It was then that she realized that the miracle had happened. Unless there had been mix-ups on cueing and entering, on exits and crossings before she had run upstairs— and she did not fancy that there had been—the timing had been perfect. How? It was impossible.

She had planned the way she would excuse that inevitable roughness later. "After all, we had only four days' rehearsal. You know how these parish things are." But there would be no need for that.

Then she heard footsteps outside—heavy footsteps. A man's voice. Oh. It was Father Cooney's.

"Nope. Can't find her at all. She's just disappeared!"

She was safe here. To think. To wait. Idly she picked up the program, flipping through it. So many patrons! Snob appeal and shame. What a way! And so many dragooned advertisers, the poor things.

On the front page she saw it. They had no right to do that!

DIRECTED BY SISTER GERVAISE.

Even on her own programs her name never appeared. And this wasn't her play. This wasn't the kind of thing she stood for at all. Now she *was* furious.

Her fury carried her on nicely through most of the second part. She was particularly annoyed because it was really very good.

The only disappointment was that when the finale came, with its tribute to Father Cooney, he had disappeared, slipping off in darkness toward the stage with the tall man who had arrived late. Too bad. He should have heard the audience cheer; how, by a stroke of genius, Mr. Morrison had got them all to join in, so that the lights went up on a singing crowd, standing and serenading the pastor. Very jolly indeed.

Then Mr. Morrison waved them into silence.

"Ladies and gentlemen," he began, "I have a great announcement for you. But first of all, I want you to know that this show was directed by a wonderful little nun we have here right among us, and who has never heard the appreciation we all feel for her. She's done a lot for our sons and daughters and I want to go on record she's done a lot for me, too, and for all of us. You can read her name on the program, because we knew she'd come through for us . . ."

Of course. Why hadn't she seen that part? The program had been printed before she stepped in at all. How could they have known what she'd do? She had had no intention . . .

". . . and more than that! Tonight we have the signal honor of having with us to view our great extravaganza, as Sister Gervaise calls it, no other than one whose name is known to all: a great actor, a great gentleman, an adornment of the American stage and of the Catholic Church, that illustrious man who has done us the honor of flying from his recent triumphs in St. Louis to be with her and us. He also has an announcement. I give you Sister Gervaise's father, Richard Rhodes."

Oh dear! Oh wonderful! Please God, let my dad be perfectly sober. O dear God, don't let him tell any Irish jokes! Oh, thank you, dear Lord—no wonder the back was familiar—I'm so glad to see him.

He spoke very simply. Yes, he had let some gray show over his temples. The toupee was faultless, but they would all think of her hereafter as a very young girl indeed to have such a young father. Goodness. She was almost forty. He was, she knew, sixty-one.

"I'm very glad to be here," he said. "My daughter has told me a good deal about you. But it warms my heart to know what you really think about her.

"We Irish," he continued (why, that rascal—he didn't have a drop of Irish blood in him), "we Irish may be a sentimental lot, but I must tell you that I never saw anything my daughter did that warmed the cockles of my heart more than this wonderful piece tonight. I want to tell you sincerely that it's the best thing she has ever done!"

Applause. Oh, don't say that! Please, Dad. Don't get carried away. You're on the wrong side. This isn't the kind of thing I want them to learn from me! And precious little of my work you've ever seen anyway, you old dear.

"But I do not say this in compliment to my girl. I say that she couldn't have done less with the really wonderful talent she had to work with." He turned to the players. "Even I couldn't direct you badly!" They laughed, properly. He put his arm around Stanley and—no, it couldn't be! Theresa!

Not Rosemary, not Margaret, Theresa! Maybe she was just nearest. But no, he meant it. "And any time you two want a job in my plays, you can have them."

Wild cheers then.

He let Stanley go but he kept holding hands with Theresa.

"Yet there is one more thing. I know that you came here not only to honor our great patron saint, but to pay particular tribute to your pastor. My daughter has told me much about him, and, from what I hear, I have a strong presentiment that he spoils her."

How little you know!

"However, although it is my first time to meet him, I can understand how his great, generous Irish heart leads him into that beautiful failing—to spoil you all. And now, in good time, his great gifts of learning and sanctity have been recognized—yes—by the Holy See itself. And although he has told me, out of his deep humility, that he hopes you will always call him and think of him as Father, I now present to you—The Very Reverend Monsignor Cooney!"

Monsignor! Mrs. Morrison had known. What didn't she know?

The Monsignor came on, resplendent in purple. No wonder the poor man had wanted a special fete this night. How glad she was that she had helped. And, by the way, who was the better showman? Her father, the professional, or Monsignor Cooney in his purple?

Who was the better showman? What was this she was thinking? Her father's manner had been perfect. It was superb acting. Yet, was it too perfect? What was the difference between his professional manner, and that of these people who had performed tonight? Was this a silly thing they had done, or was it more real somehow, more authentic? She would not be false to the ideals of great drama, and yet—here she was wondering.

This came out of the people. A good thing.

And later, backstage, when her father said to her, "I meant that. It was the best thing you've ever done," she had replied, "Just a few moments ago I was tempted to think so, but I rejected it as a bad thought."

"The timing," he said, "the timing was wonderful. How did you do it?"

"I don't know. It was a miracle."

Behind them Mr. Morrison laughed. "I'll show you. You see, we couldn't get all that in the rehearsals we had, so—well, I thought up a little scheme. Got it from TV."

He pointed up behind the arch. On either side were rollers, connecting a tremendously long strip of paper. On it were cues for everything. All the actors had had to do was to look up and read what they were to do next. The two men on the ladders had clung there all evening, unrolling the cue sheet.

"Genius!" her father had said. "That's the way the theatre is born!"

"You're wonderful," Sister Gervaise applauded. "Why, it even kept them from looking down at their feet the way they always do. I wondered . . ."

"You're pretty wonderful yourself," Mr. Morrison said. They were, she noticed, a bit withdrawn now from the knots of people on the stage. And Mr. Morrison, oddly enough, was looking really shy, embarrassed, like a small boy. He was very serious. "I was thinking . . . would it be bad manners . . . if I was to ask you . . ."

She smiled at him, said nothing, and felt stagey doing it.

101

". . . if I could come over to the convent and talk to you? I got something real serious on my mind."

"Is it about Rosemary?"

"Sort of."

"I'm glad to see any of my girls' fathers. Will Mrs. Morrison be with you?"

"Does she have to?"

"Not really."

"Then I guess maybe not, if it'd be all right."

"Tomorrow?"

"Maybe about seven."

"Good."

She turned back to discover her father looking at his watch.

"What are you doing?" she asked him. "You are going to stay a few days, aren't you?"

He shook his head. He looked old now. "No. Have to catch the midnight to get a plane out of Milwaukee for Boston."

"Tonight?"

"Mm mm."

She did not remonstrate with him. It was the pattern. It had always been so, as far back as she could remember. Never any home. Never any permanence.

"Got to run away right now."

"I know. And you know I wish you could stay."

"So do I. Do you pray for me?"

"All the time."

"I need it. And you? Are you happy?"

"Very happy."

"I knew it. You see, you've got a home." He pointed out toward the people. And yes, he was right. She had a home.

He kissed her lightly and turned away, then back again. "By the way, I meant that about that little girl. What's her name?"

"Theresa?"

"You bet. She's got it. Good night!"

Theresa? Did she? Had she been so close to Theresa that she couldn't tell any more? Just today she had been wishing there was only one of her students who had the real thing. Now she was not so sure she wanted it for them. Theresa?

Stanley came up to say good night and thank you. She did not say much to him, but her hand on his arm was congratulation. She led him over to the fire-escape door and together, boy and nun, they looked down upon the retreating figure of Richard Rhodes.

Her mind was saying strange things to the boy:

I'm glad you're not going to grow up. Because you have the thing—the thing I'm glad I gave away. Because I have a home. And so will you. But if you did grow up, you wouldn't, you know. You'd have to go off night after night, like that. You'd have to live in his world. And I wouldn't want that for you, little Stanislaus.

Her father's boyish stride faltered when he thought he could no longer be seen, and he disappeared into the wintry, snow-clad street.

But because it was St. Patrick's Day and because it was March, there came then, even through the night, the first mild breath of spring.

Chapter 8

M R. MORRISON was waiting in the parlor as he had promised. In a way it was too bad, because it broke up the recreation just when it was beginning to be fun. First the nuns
had started planning what they could do for the new monsignor, but no one was really in a mood for any earnestness
and soon they were having a "revue" of their own.

Sister Drusilda showed surprising talent. No one had
known it before, but she had a large repertory of comic
Irish songs that she sang with a perfectly frozen face and
in a quavering soprano that was definitely doleful. Mother
Dolorosa was persuaded, for the thousandth time, to con-
tribute "Little White Lies."

"Oh, you've all heard that!"

They all had, but they listened again with relish.

Yet it was Sister Inez whose dance won the prize. She
had fashioned herself a fan from the diocesan weekly, and,
though she did not stir from her chair, she managed, sitting
down, to give a completely realistic impression of dancing
a fandango. Even the dog Lady got excited. Lady worshiped
Sister Inez.

Just in the middle of it, Mr. Morrison had come.

"It's not about Rosemary," he had said after many false
starts. "It's about my wife mainly."

She should have suspected that. Perhaps she had. Too often Rosemary's accounts had dealt with a divided authority.

He went on, "Of course, it bothers the kid. She's pretty much upset the way things are going. You know how it is, when things aren't right at home."

"I think so," she said. But really, she did not know. How could she know about a home? Her father had idolized her mother until the day she died, and, on his infrequent sojourns to where his family happened to be at any given time, had positively paid court to her. But a home? Not till now.

"I mean, my wife's a wonderful woman. Don't get me wrong. Say! Should I be telling you all this?"

"I think maybe you should. If it will do any good. But why me? I don't even know Mrs. Morrison very well."

"Yeah. That's why I picked on you. I had to talk to a woman—but not just any woman, see? And a lot of you nuns know my wife pretty well. They'd think I was crazy. But you're different. What'll I do, Sister?"

She smiled at him. "You remind me of the old fellow who went to the doctor, and when he was asked what his symptoms were, he said, 'That's your business. Find them out!'" Mr. Morrison looked puzzled. "You haven't told me very much, I mean. I'll have to have more to go on."

He told her then, and she could reconstruct that home life pretty well. There was no doubt from his recountal that Mrs. Morrison had made her point, fairly early in their wedded life, that she had married beneath herself, and her husband had accepted it unquestioningly. He was a Babbitt. He could make money, and that was about it. He was a good-time Charlie with the boys, he said, but he never could keep up with his wife's talk about the *Seven Storey Moun-*

tain and all like that. Oh, he went to Communion with the men every second Sunday, but all this other business—and the books Sister Emily gave Mrs. Morrison! He had tried one once. It was by a woman named Juliana of Norwich. Ever hear of her?

To get back, though. Everything had gone fine when Rosemary came along. It was only recently, since Rosemary had grown up, that her parents' views had at last put a barrier between them.

"It isn't as though we both didn't want the best for her. Only my best and the Missus'—they're different. I just want her to be a nice, ordinary girl, you know—a lot of boys hanging around, sure. But just because old Doc Maguire's got a lot of things I wish I had, I don't see why it has to be young Joe all the time. Do you?"

"I thought Rosemary liked Joe."

"She likes him all right. He's a fine kid. But don't you think she ought to play the field?"

"That's exactly what I think. They all should."

Mr. Morrison looked relieved; he also looked like a man who seldom encountered agreement. "Well, see. First there was this Nick Collasanto. Rosemary liked him."

"She did? I never noticed . . ."

"How could you? Mrs. M. put her foot down. She's got a way. She just says it once, then she never even will talk about it again. That isn't like a woman, is it?"

Sister Gervaise laughed. "It's like some women."

"That so? See what I don't know? Well, anyway, Rosemary switched over to Joe, and that's O.K. with the missus. Then, after that, along came this business about college and what-all. You know about that. I don't want her to get any fancy education. Just, you know, regular. See what I mean? Like Marycliff."

Let it pass. Don't even show annoyance. He means well. But why did they all secretly feel that Marycliff was just a cut below other places? There was nothing the matter with Marycliff. It was a grade-A college, or definitely would be once the Board of Examiners got around to giving their final word.

"I see what you mean," she said. "And I think you're right, holding out for a Catholic education. That is your main reason, isn't it?"

"Oh sure. Certainly. But Mrs. M., she says Rosemary's had twelve years of the nuns and nobody's going to make her into anything but a Catholic. She says she thinks it helps a girl to bump up against things outside. Besides, they got a swell Newman Club there where she wants her to go."

"I know." She had heard all the arguments. She could prompt the givers of them. By the time they got through, you would think the choice of a pagan education was made for the sheer love of God.

"That ain't all. *Isn't*," he amended. "You know what? You know what she wants to do?"

Sister Gervaise did not know what Mrs. Morrison wanted to do.

"She's got an idea in her head. She's got a cousin East, near Yonkers somewhere. She wants to go and stay there so's to be near Rosemary."

"What will you do?"

"Me? I stay here. I got my business in West Alis. What can I do?"

"You stay here all alone? Why, that's fantastic!"

"Yeah. That's what I said. I got mad one night—she never

gets mad. She just doesn't say anything. Not even when she's hopping. It isn't natural."

That was true. The incident of the gray chiffon dress. Not one word about it, not even an acknowledgment of Sister Gervaise's sincere note of apology. Quite a technique that lady had. It had kept Sister Gervaise on tenterhooks for weeks, wondering when something would be said. How would that affect anyone, carried over years?

"What did you say?"

"I shouldn't of said what I did. I told her she wanted things both ways. See? We're Catholics, I mean kind of special Catholics—at least my wife is. You know, she'd just as soon think of divorce as, well, being a cannibal. But this way, it'd be all right. She could live East—she always wanted to live East—and everybody'd think it was all copacetic, with Rosemary there and all. So I says to her, 'Why don't you make it complete? Why don't you go to Reno?' "

"What did she say?"

"Nothing. She never said a word. Just went on with the plans, just like that."

"When was this?"

"Oh—just a while ago. Just before Lent."

The day Rosemary had come to ask about changing to another school? Of course. That was the trouble with the young, they blew up the problem, were torn by it, but their solutions almost always tended only to make matters worse. How could they be so clear on one thing and not on the other? The things they proposed to do! Unless, of course, they changed their minds, or, more probably, simply forgot about their previous preposterous schemes.

"I think I know something about that. That was the time Rosemary was so upset."

108 ☞

"Did she tell you?"

"No. Rosemary never really talks to me."

"She don't? She trusts you a lot."

"Does she? I'd never know."

"Yeah. That's not too good. She clams up—just like her mother."

But yet, what could the child do? The two persons most important in the world, the father whom she adored, the mother whose superiority she had learned to accept, had given her, all her life probably, exactly contrary advice. It was a wonder she wasn't more mixed up than she was.

There was a silence between them. In the distance the compline bell rang.

"What'll I do?" Mr. Morrison asked. "You name it."

She liked talking to men. You just said it, out with it, and you didn't have to worry.

"Be a man. Put your foot down. Just tell your wife Rosemary is going to Marycliff. Then use her tactics. Don't discuss it any more."

Mr. Morrison rose. He towered above her, looking down at her with the bewildered and hurt expression of a St. Bernard.

"It won't work," he said. "It's too late." And then, stammering like a schoolboy, he said, "You see—I love my wife."

Later, Sister Consolata was totally uncomprehending and not a little amazed when Sister Gervaise whispered to her, "Love! I hate love!"

The whole community was to remember the night after St. Patrick's Day as, for some unknown reason, the last of their jolly recreations. They had had such a good time.

But then Sister Consolata became engrossed in her preparations for the Holy Week music. Sister Drusilda, who for a long time now had been asking for funds to meet the rising cost of living and had been constantly refused, became even more bothered because the provincial motherhouse had increased its tax, and she just couldn't make ends meet. Mother Dolorosa had developed a springtime hacking cough and had refused to stay in bed more than two days. Several of the younger nuns had banded together, almost, but not quite, of course, into a clique, and played Chinese checkers every evening. Sister Emily seemed to be constantly in the parlor advising Mrs. Morrison, and even Mother Bernardine, usually most careful about common life, seemed withdrawn into herself.

Indeed she was. She had at last written the Bishop saying that they could not possibly take care of Father Fleury's summer school. She had received a rather strained letter from the chancellor, intimating His Excellency's displeasure. And what made it worse was that, of all times, she knew she had chosen the worst time to be at outs with the hierarchy. Because something that she dreaded was about to happen to her.

As a result, she would sit quite alone some evenings, with only the dog beside her. That is, Lady would be beside her if Sister Inez were not about. Lady, they all thought, was very intelligent and was aware that Sister Inez detested dogs. Particularly dogs that shed. And Lady was resolved to win over Sister Inez by shedding on her constantly.

"That ah-nee-mahl!" Sister Inez cried. "She moults!"

Yes. There was something wrong. You couldn't put your finger on it. And it wasn't just last-quarter fatigue either, because it continued after the Easter recess, when they should have been rested.

There was the day when Sister Roseanne, troubled about the imminence of her full vows, shooed Lady away and said to Sister Gervaise, "That dog! If it's the Superior's dog, why doesn't she train it better?" Then she added what no better formed Sister would ever say. "Sometimes I think Reverend Mother is more interested in that old dog than she is in her community."

You couldn't be sure, of course, but Sister Gervaise had thought that Mother Bernardine overheard, as indeed she had.

Strange, how the tensions grew. Even the rehearsals for *Murder in the Cathedral* were not so joyous as they should have been. The students didn't like the play; they didn't understand it; they hankered after the fleshpots of the St. Patrick's Day extravaganza, and Mr. MacGill constantly reminded her that on that night of nights the men had put the chairs back right. She wished that they had made just one tiny mistake.

A strange sense of suspension, as if something were about to happen, was in the air. But nothing was happening. The Morrisons made no move; the Theresa-Joe-Rosemary triangle remained the same.

Only her classes gave her joy. In April her students always welded themselves together, and it was a yearly miracle that she loved and rejoiced in. Things that had been far beyond them in September now seemed child's play. They could not understand why they had wanted to resign from her classes back in the fall. She could feel them growing, like spring things in the sunshine.

Then one day in early April she met Margaret Fleming who was looking at the empty niche.

"We're going to fill that niche for you, Sister. The alumnae gift this year. And I'll tell you a secret."

"Wonderful! I'm so glad. What's the secret?"

"You know that artist in Sheraton you used to tell us about all the time?"

"Felix Alemando? He's magnificent."

"We got him to design the statue. Just for you."

"You're grand! He's a great artist." She knew his madonna would have no roses on her feet.

"It'll be ready to look at—the model—in just a week or two. Then we'll unveil it May 30."

"That's just fine! I can't tell you how much I appreciate that. You know I thought you'd forgotten about me."

"Why?"

"Do you know how many weeks it is since you were around to see me? I don't even know how things are going with you and Jim. You haven't told me anything."

Margaret was distressed. "There's nothing to tell."

"No?"

And Margaret summed up the vacancies of the last weeks. "That's the trouble," she said, "there's just nothing to tell."

Chapter 9

Sɪsᴛᴇʀ Gᴇʀᴠᴀɪsᴇ wanted to say, "I don't care either."

That would be classroom heresy and she couldn't very well admit to that. She had asked herself long ago about the values of what she was teaching and she really knew the answers. But with Nick Collasanto's tone, if not his words, indicating a rebellious disinterest in the date of Shakespeare's birth, she wondered again. After all the pleasure she had taken in this class, there would now come days like this. Restlessness and distraction among the students that echoed the restless distraction within her own mind. She was thinking, like them, of other and possibly more important things.

Their minds were on what they would do after graduation; her mind was half on the problem of her own spiritual stagnation and half on the problem of Margaret Fleming. After that last, too-hurried and unsatisfactory meeting, she had seen no more of Margaret. And now this evening she was coming with her problem.

In a way, all problems were the same. Everybody wanted something to happen. This restless generation. Unsure. But what could it be sure of? Boys facing service without warfare, their attitude summed up by Jack Murphy's reply to the question: "Are you going to college?" in answer to which he had written on the graduation form: "Ha! Ha!"

And Sister Gervaise knew it was worse for the girls. How could you teach Shakespeare to them? Just waiting. There was nothing in the books about that. And marking time. Like Margaret. And herself, wondering what the teaching of dates had to do with what the spiritual books called the ascent of the mountain of God. She really knew, of course, and yet here she was not even out of breath from the climb. She had been entirely too complacent.

Sister Gervaise's voice said, "1564. You ought to remember that. It's important." A languid fly buzzed in the west windowpane and some of the students looked at it with equal languor. Her mind was saying, "What's important about it?" and, "What shall I tell her tonight? What do I know? Who knows anything?" Margaret's trouble had come with the waiting. But everybody was waiting nowadays.

And the class was waiting, too, the nun realized. The fly dropped, flat and noiseless, to the window sill; the clock still said twenty minutes to go until the dismissal bell would ring. Sister Gervaise closed her book, resolving to be stimulating, to sell the eternal verities, to make this generation realize what it was fighting for. Waiting for.

"Some of you are going to die," she said. The class looked at her hopefully, as the congregation did at the mission sermon on hell, the one Father Montfort gave so devastatingly. "And some of you are just going to go through life waiting for something exciting to happen. But all of you are going to have to fight to keep our civilization alive. Civilization means things like Shakespeare. Like this. These truths.

These eternal verities. Because of the fact that they are true . . ."

You see, she did know, really. But despite her forced vehemence, the class was stirring in its sticky seats again. Too warm for May.

"Take the play we are studying, *Romeo and Juliet*. You know the story, and even though Mr. Powers said that people don't talk like that, people do live like that."

Then she stopped. A thought exploded in her mind. Did people live like that? Or was that the trouble? Waiting for a blinding flash of some bewildering romance, confidently expecting moonlight on a balcony; or arms raised in the form of a cross, a cry of *"Viva Christo Rey,"* a shot ringing out and a body slumping beneath a white wall. Trained to that. All the romantic tradition of modern Western culture. All the incredible tenseness of the last half-century.

Then not having anything happen. Two armies sitting beside the Maginot Line; a barrier down the midst of Berlin. Just the waiting, the worried wondering. The plodding life of St. Rita's Convent, Wolf Head, Wisconsin, U.S.A. Not behind the Iron Curtain. This, and Margaret's feeling, or lack of feeling, for Jim.

She laughed aloud and then explained to her students, taking her veiled parable from the true story of Margaret and Jim. Not at all like Romeo and Juliet. Not even like the romantic lives of the saints. As yet there was not even a conclusion, a married-and-happy-ever-after, because Margaret was coming to see her tonight and she prayed that her advice would not be as ill-fated as Friar Laurence's to Romeo. Not ended yet. But the story would last until the bell rang, and that was a blessing.

She had learned long ago that you could teach anything at all as long as it did not seem to be on the class matter and if the pupils thought you were off the subject. Well, there was Margaret as a topic.

When the bell clanged for three-thirty dismissal she was still at the romantic part, but her point was just the opposite. The class sat flatteringly, willing to hear more. Always willing to hear love stories. But she must not. Discipline. Mother Bernardine had already spoken to her about keeping her classes late. Wasn't that when there were other classes to follow? No. She would be adamant.

"That's all for now," she said, rising.

"Oh, Sister!"

"In the name of the Father and of . . ."

At the end of the prayer she gathered up her notes and books and departed before the knot of girls and the perpetual, inevitable, single boy could gather around her desk. She escaped by the door below the gym, only once glancing up the iron stairs to note that a trail of paper streamers was dripping down them and that the door to the auditorium was not locked. Things left over from the penny sale the night before. They couldn't blame her for that carelessness. Now she could hear Mr. MacGill, with the scrape of his broom like a profanity against the floor.

She thought she had escaped everyone, wanting a moment to think about Margaret and what to tell her tonight. How could she really tell her anything? She knew so few of the answers herself. Time. If only she had time to think—and to pray. Some of the Sisters said part of their rosary as they went across the asphalt pavement to the convent, but she was always distracted by the empty niche and she preferred just to think and to save her rosary for the quiet, after lights out. Yet usually, even in these few moments, she was pursued by the youngsters.

This time she had eluded them. No. Not quite. But it did not matter. It was only Theresa. Sister Gervaise performed the daily ritual of inquiring after Theresa's health, which was uniformly excellent even when Charlie had the mumps. She went into chapel. She had half an hour for herself before rehearsal time for the graduation play. Five minutes here. That was all.

She scolded herself for self-indulgence because it was always more than five minutes. Ten, some prostrate days. Yet one of her retreat resolutions had been not to delude herself into thinking that the rest she found in prayer was more pleasing to God than preparations for her assigned duties. She must be on her guard against the devil who came to her as an angel of light.

As she knelt there, the same impatience that had bothered her recently filled all her prayer. She felt herself struggling toward something, some greater union with God, some assurance that she was not just marking time.

"Dear Lord," she prayed, "let me grow in your love. Let me not just stagnate in the daily grind. Let me at least be sure that what I do for you is not half for myself, but really for you. Let me be sure!"

How could you be sure?

Wearily, at last, she rose, genuflected, went to her cell. As usual, the first thing that struck her was the holy card that Laura McElroy had sent her on the day that Laura had taken her vows. Sister Gervaise had intended to destroy it. It was sentimental and indicated an attachment. But it had meant so much: her only vocation. The other nuns had so many vocations, like scalps at their girdles, but it seemed girls interested in drama weren't attracted to the convent. So it meant a good deal that Laura, whom she had had in the old days before she went to Catholic School of the Theatre, whose high-school romances she had shepherded, whose vocation she had defended against a tearful mother, had not only entered but persevered. Very happy. Doing good work. One of those illustrious beings, a college nun, teaching at the Cliffs.

Sister Gervaise let the card stay.

Hastily she took her script book from the plain wooden rack on her desk. Sister Emily had smoothed and linseed-oiled hers. It looked nice. Someday she would get around to doing that herself.

Come, now. No woolgathering. Cut a speech on page 76. The pastor might not like it. Why couldn't she advance in prayer like Sister Emily? Margaret. Margaret must marry Jim. Ridiculous to be unsure. I wish marriage were a lake I could throw her into. Mother Bernardine said the exams had to be typed by Tuesday. This is Monday. Script book. Page 76. Let me see. Here. Jack Murphy is really getting out of hand. All boys restless. What was the matter with Nick? Something on Rosemary's mind, too. Mary, Mother of Divine Mercy, help them. Let me see. What could replace this speech?

"Living and partially living . . . between the . . ." Change to: "Would I were a glove upon that hand."

Ridiculous. Romeo and Juliet. Too much romanticism. Change to . . .

The girls were worse off than the boys; the boys at least were going to do something; the girls just waited. No. Write this in. Write the new speech in. What would Mr. Eliot say? Was it a violation of copyright? At least she wasn't doing what she knew some religious did: stealing a play, changing the name, putting it on without any rights. She didn't approve of that. But write in a new speech?

The seventeen minutes were over.

The rehearsal consumed all her energies until six twenty-two and, for a change, the dinner reading was interesting. At recreation, of course, you had to follow the conversation, and, although recreations had taken a turn for the better now that they met out-of-doors under the arbors where the little buds were like kids' horns and the filtered green of the evening crept about you, it was easy to lose the thread of the conversation. You caught snatches, tried to piece them together.

"I don't know what's come over the lot of them. Can't make them study."

"I certainly hope the diocesan exams aren't as mixed up as they were last year . . ."

"We ought to have a new house at Sheboygan. I was talking to Mother Provincial and she said . . ."

"At least I'm glad we had the radio for the Democratic convention. It was nice of Mrs. Morrison to send it over . . ."

"How is the play coming, Sister?"

Margaret. "What?"

"I asked how the play was coming."

"Fine. Just fine. You know at this stage . . ."

Margaret and Jimmy. Romeo and Juliet. Her own soul and the love of God.

"Isn't it grand about Bishop Sheen? The book salesman told me just the other day that Jews and Protestants and everybody . . ."

Then the bell, and it was almost eight before the nuns were through with Compline. The waxed parlor was nearly dark before Sister Gervaise got there. She switched on the light. It was pitiless. Margaret's brown eyes were dead, as if she had stared too long at space, or across long distances.

"I thought you would never come," Margaret said.

"I wasn't long. We were in chapel."

"I heard you. At first it was beautiful. But then it seemed so—so endless."

"I should think you would be used to waiting."

"You never get used to waiting. You can get used to something, but not to nothing."

"You learned that at the Cliffs."

"It's true."

"Yes," Sister Gervaise said, with a conviction deeper than Margaret could understand, "it is true." She seated herself on the lumpy chair so that Margaret could have the other one. The light from the center bracket remained unmerciful, making Margaret's bright hair seem dull and dead. "You always want to do something, don't you?" the nun went on. She was thinking of how her confessor had instructed her when she complained that she was just marking time in the spiritual life and that maybe that was what God wanted. "Maybe waiting's what God wants," she said.

"He may have wanted it before, but He doesn't now," Margaret said. "Now He wants a decision. And I can't make it. I made one a long time ago. When I agreed to marry Jim. Then I waited. I kept my word. Now I just don't know what to do."

"Why?"

"I don't love him—I think."

Sister Gervaise smiled. "I like that 'I think.' That helps. Tell me about it if you want to."

Margaret told her, picking up the threads from the last time she had been at the convent, shortly before Jim came home, when she had been worried about what she would find or he would find in her. But he had been the same Jim, only stronger, better looking, kinder. And so patient. That was the trouble. So terribly patient. There had been only once, the time of the St. Patrick's Day play . . .

"It wasn't a play."

. . . when he had seemed at all romantic.

"I don't know how to tell you exactly," she said. "I don't think I'm expecting to be swept off my feet. Only there ought to be something. More than I have. I just like him a lot. And I admire him. I don't want to hurt him. You couldn't find a better man in the world than Jim Dugan. I know all that right up here in my mind. I can say all the words, but nothing happens. Sometimes I ask myself what I am looking for."

Sister Gervaise knew that the complete answer to that question could not be given now. She had found it in St. Augustine. But what were they looking for here and now in this generation? The great adventure, the high emotion, the spiritual ecstasy. Never the long climb, the steady pull. But there was still one possibility she must explore.

"Do you remember the play we did before I went to CST?" All her life was thus divided into two parts: before and after CST. Margaret and Laura, before; Rosemary and Theresa, after. "It was by Thornton Wilder."

"*Our Town?* Oh yes. It's a honey."

"There was a scene in it. It is the night before the wedding. Everything is ready. Then the little bride gets frightened. She discovers that she doesn't want to leave home and go away with a strange man."

"Yes. And she wonders what they are ever going to talk about for so many years to come. I remember. It's perfect."

"And it's true. Could it be true of you?"

Margaret considered for a moment. Her honey-colored eyebrows puckered, with smooth furrows between them.

"No," she said at length. "At least not totally. Maybe a little. But you see it isn't the night before the wedding. If it were, it would be all right. If we had got married right away when Joe came home. But now we have to wait again. Money. A job. All those things. He's so practical now. Maybe, though, I am frightened. Maybe everybody is."

"Maybe everybody is frightened." Sister Gervaise looked back into the past. The night before her clothing, with her own wedding dress ready for the divine espousals and every reason in the world to be happy. And how, just before lights out, she had caught a glimpse of the dress and had realized, with a quick indrawing of breath, that this was the fatal step. There really had not even been a temptation, just a sudden fear of putting off the old and putting on the new. She had laughed at herself, telling herself that this is what she wanted more than anything in the world. But then she had thought of the two years of novitiate that lay ahead. If only her final vows were tomorrow, sealed and ratified. But two years. And the moment's revulsion had been real.

Margaret had relaxed a bit now. "That has something to do with it, I guess. But it's more. It's just—how can you be sure you're in love?"

How can you be sure of your vocation? How can you be sure you're doing God's will? How can you be sure you are advancing up the mountain of perfection, as the mystical writers put it? Sure of anything? Sister Gervaise could almost hear the litany of questions coming from a thousand lips, as if all the world were asking. Certainty. The need to be sure.

"Thank God for the Apostles' Creed and the Articles of Faith," she said. "Blessed be dogma."

"What do you mean? You always say such tantalizing things."

"I mean, at least *we* have something we can be sure of. That's a start on the road. And other things? God gave us minds. Not perfect, maybe, but capable of finding us some certainty."

Margaret laughed. "But there's one thing I always thought you would be certain about. Wouldn't you think anybody would know when they were in love? It sounds sort of silly to be confused about that, doesn't it?"

"How did you expect to know?"

"The way other girls do; the way they talk about their boy friends. Even the way they look."

"Teenagers! I've heard most of the words. To listen to Theresa Doyle you'd think she was full of purple passion. That is, when I'm not around, or she doesn't think I am. Have you exchanged personalities with them? Or maybe, what's worse, they're working up their feelings to what they think they ought to be. I hate synthetic emotions— particularly offstage." She stopped, smiled. "That was quite a speech, wasn't it? But you do think you're missing something they have. I understand that. And just how do you feel?"

"Oh, I like Jim a lot! We never have to worry about what we're going to talk about. We always have plenty."

"What do you talk about?"

"Books, plays, church. What we're going to buy for the house. Old times at school. Things like that. Everything."

"That's pretty good for a start. And tell me—how about other boys? Can you talk about everything with them?"

"Why—why, I guess not. It's different with Jim. I never have to think about what I'm going to say. I just feel sort of comfortable. That isn't enough, is it?"

Sister Gervaise wanted to cry out that it was tremendously enough, but you couldn't say that to a girl who had been fed, as they all were, on romantic traditions. No. She wouldn't know what was meant. All the nun did was to ask another question.

"How do you feel about him when he isn't around?"

"Honestly, I don't miss him much. I'm glad to see him, of course, but I'm just glad. I call downstairs, 'Just a minute,' and he looks at television until I'm ready. Sometimes, Sister, I don't hurry very much. That's mean, isn't it? I'm so sure he'll be there. He's so sort of *permanent*."

"Not very exciting, is he?" The nun remembered how exciting Jim had seemed once, going off in uniform, and how exciting he had sounded in the letters from Korea. And now she could just see Jim resting, with his feet up on the ottoman, half-listening to suds ads on TV. Always there. And Margaret, disturbed because she didn't miss him, when she knew he would be dropping around night after night anyway, poking at the dials of the set again, waiting for her, while she didn't hurry much. Margaret had waited for him so long.

"Maybe your missingness is all used up," the nun went on. "You did miss him. Do you remember?"

"Oh yes. That was better, but I don't now. Not the way I ought to."

"How ought you to? I mean, how do you expect to feel? The way the other girls do?"

"Shouldn't I?"

"No."

"Why?"

"You're not any other girl. You're Margaret. She's different. You have never even read yourself in a book. It hasn't been written yet because you have never happened before. I feel terribly sorry for you."

"Why, whatever do you mean?" The girl's dark eyes were puzzled. She had not expected this kind of pity.

"I'm terribly sorry for the new girls all over the country. We've trained you to excitement, even how to be brave in crises, and we've blared terribly stimulating things at you all your lives. Then we make you just sit. Just wait. We never told you how to do that. We never said a single word to you about the wonderful blessing of calm. And the virtue of that comfortable feeling. We've made you expect great big emotions and, God knows, we have given you tremendous events. But we were so wrong. I think it's just too bad for people to have done things like this to you."

"Who?"

"Myself, somewhat. Every day in class. Always in drama rehearsals. I share the blame. I've hated to drill and been afraid to be boring. And the other people are the same way. Writers and poets and Hollywood and the comic books even. They all let you down when the lovely, smooth, solid thing comes to you. As a result, you're missing life!"

"Who, me?"

"Yes. And your whole generation." And then Sister Gervaise committed the heresy of her life. She said what had been trembling on her lips since this afternoon. She said, "I'm mad at Shakespeare."

Margaret laughed. "Coming from you, that's something."

"I know. But he isn't fair to you. Romeo and Juliet, indeed! Here you are in love with Jim . . ."

"I'm not sure."

"Then get sure. You're not Juliet and he isn't Romeo. You're Margaret. And you're having one of the fine experiences of life and you don't even know it. You do love Jim. I'm not Friar Laurence, thank God, but I know something about love."

Sister Gervaise saw the incredulity on Margaret's face, as if she wanted to ask what they all wanted to: "How do you know? You're a nun." And how could you tell them that one day you, too, with the fears folded away, had gone down to your espousals, and a ring had been placed on your finger, and the deep, beautiful peace had come that all the surface troubles in the world had never taken away? How could you say that maybe you, too, had missed the realization of that peace, wanting something more, different, and had not known how wonderful it had been, this profound, comforting sense, until right now. Missing your life, too. Missing the marvel of your love. How could you say that?

The girl would only turn to you in disbelief. "But that's different. That's loving God." As if the love of God taught you nothing at all.

"I do know," Sister Gervaise went on, "that when two people can talk about the same things, when they admire each other, when they like to be together, when they feel a special sort of comfort they don't find in anybody else, when one is confident that the other will always be waiting, when one has waited through a kind of awfulness as you have, I know that's something pretty wonderful. I would call it love."

"But it isn't . . ."

"No. It isn't the balcony scene. It just happens to be the

way Margaret loves Jim. It's the way most people in other ages of the world knew they were in love. It's the grand, deep-down thing. Look, girl, don't be searching for something you haven't got. Oh, it's all right if you have it. I hear it's quite delightful. But if you can't have it, then thank God for the things you do have. Put a value on the experiences God gives you."

"How can I do that?"

Now out of her new confidence, out of the answer to her prayers for assurance, Sister Gervaise spoke.

"Say to yourself: There never in the world before has been another Jim. There never has been another I. This year has never rolled around until now. Out of all eternity, this is it. And no matter what I have read or heard, the fables have been about other people on another day. Never before, since the world began, has our love been."

As the nun watched silently, she saw the old, sure expression coming back. She saw lips moving as if in prayer, repeating what she had heard. "Never before since the world began has *our* love been." She saw someone ready now for the new adventure, the brave facing of the modern world. Her world. And Sister Gervaise thanked God.

"That is beautiful," Margaret said. "I will never forget it."

"It is truer than the poets."

"It is poetry. But—how did you know, Sister?"

Sister Gervaise rose and walked with Margaret to the door. Almost flippantly she said, "Oh, I read a lot of books. But I got that answer by rejecting most of them. All but one."

Then when Margaret was gone, Sister Gervaise went into the chapel at last and knowing that her prayer was answered she knelt in thanksgiving. She had read it in a book. She reviewed the pages again, recalling the impatience of her postulancy, when it had seemed that she could not wait for her clothing in the habit of religion; she remembered the aching moments of consolation when it had seemed to her that her heart would break with the joy of living in the household of God. Then the long, dry period of novitiate when, though she did not waver, all the joy had departed and she had gone on mechanically doing her daily tasks, not daring to count the hours. And the months. And the long months. And the two years.

Then there had been this life, with no sensible consolation at all, no sense of advance, so many people, so much work, and at last almost a certainty that she did not love God at all.

Now she knew. This year they were not making saints like the ones she had read about and admired. They had lived in different worlds and had different graces suited to their times. But God asked her to live in this world. To sanctify it somehow. To make of all distractions and drudgery and lack of time a holy thing, an offering of love.

Tomorrow, she realized, she could finish the story she had been telling her class as she could not have finished it for the restless youngsters today. Blessings even upon the bell. She would tell them of the holiness of the life that was theirs, day by day, in the unadventurous pattern of God.

So Sister Gervaise looked up at the outstretched, pinioned arms of the Crucified, who now, that the passion was over, remained thus forever, unmoving, nailed to a cross, and there on it was saving the world. And she realized then what she had known these many years, all through her religious life—in what book she had read the patient mystery of love.

Chapter 10

IT WAS DURING THIS TIME that the rumors had begun to fly. They had all realized for years that there was nothing like a convent once the rumors began. What caused them, how they flared up, what ultimately made them die, no one would ever know, but every once in a while the things would get started and there was nothing you could do about it.

The first rumor that came to Sister Gervaise was that Sister Emily was to take over dramatics. She fancied that she knew how that had started—a long time ago, when Mother Bernardine had suggested that she have a helper, and the thought of Sister Emily had crossed her mind. Although she could not remember it, she just might have voiced her suspicions to someone, unless there were mind readers around. Sometimes she thought there were.

Nothing had happened in the meantime. Once, Mother Bernardine had said something to her about not entering the boys' dressing room, as if she had ever dreamed of it; then she had remembered helping little Stanley to get ready for the extravaganza and she had explained about his being such a little boy. Mother Bernardine had said that little boys grow up, but she had known that this little boy would not grow up.

There had been no other sign of dissatisfaction, yet Sister

Consolata, in an outburst of loyalty, was indignant at the very idea and told her that everybody knew that Emily was to replace her. Nobody else could do the job with dramatics, least of all Sister Emily! Sister Gervaise smiled. As if it mattered! As if she wouldn't be glad! Of course she would.

Then there was the rumor that started just before Reverend Mother went on retreat. Superiors' retreat was early that year because there was going to be a Council, but no one knew that, or was supposed to. Although how could you miss it when everybody was aware that Mother Mount Carmel, the Provincial, was at the end of her six years of office? According to canon law, she would have to be changed, wouldn't she?

That wouldn't affect St. Rita's, Sister Gervaise said. Thank God, Mother Bernardine had two years to go. They were lucky to have her. She was a good Superior.

Then that young Sister Roseanne had said, "Oh, I don't know." While she had hastened to correct the impression by adding that a change was often good, she had said it, hadn't she? The words were out, and a rumor was seeded. Sister Gervaise had been quite sharp when she replied, "You don't know when you are well off."

Everybody liked Mother. Or at least, she amended, everybody had liked Mother. So very much. Why, she could remember the time when Sister Consolata had said, "I'm afraid about Obedience. It's so much safer if you don't *like* the Superior. Then you know that your will is being crossed and you're doing God's will. But if you get along as well as we do, I get scared maybe we're just doing things to please Reverend Mother."

That had been not so many months ago.

Everybody had liked Mother. What had happened? For

the life of her Sister Gervaise could not see any difference in Mother's attitude. She was perfectly just and she was tolerant and she had a sense of humor. Even when she got after you, you knew she was right. What did you want in a human being anyway?

She wondered, too, if Mother Bernardine perceived the change in attitude. If she did not, it would be amazing, particularly on the day she returned from retreat.

There had been nothing disrespectful, certainly not, in their welcome of her, but the old warmth and flurry were not there. She must have sensed it the moment she entered the garden enclosure where her nuns were at recreation, because their quick, bright laughter stopped suddenly as if a tension had come to them, as if their relaxation during her absence had immediately ceased. Yes. They had been glad she had been away, and their laughter stopped.

She had heard the laughter, of course, from the other side of the rhododendrons, the laughter that had always warmed her. "Hear the laughter of nuns," she had said in happier days, "and you will know what it means in the litanies when we call Our Lady the 'Cause of Our Joy.'" Could she say that now?

Sister Emily's worsted yarn fell, unraveling on the lawn. She hesitated, gave a little birdlike flutter and was down after it.

"You don't have to kneel to me," Mother Bernardine had called out.

She had intended it to be funny, Sister Gervaise knew. They all knew it also, but the titter that ran around the community was a polite appreciation of a Mother Superior's wit. Under it she could almost hear a thought, a whisper, "Oh, don't we, though?"

What was the matter with them? Mother Bernardine hesitated on the edge of the circle. Her own heart was crying out to them, how they were the best community in the world, how much she had missed them, how proud she had been of them when she had heard other Superiors talking about their subjects—not uncharitably, mind you, but with a just tinge of supernatural envy for the life of the nuns at her St. Rita's. And now she knew that it had been presumptuous of her to have renewed her constant retreat resolutions, to avoid self-satisfaction in her popularity. For years she had tried to conquer it. Now, perhaps, God had heard her prayers and had taken it away from her. But how? Why?

Mother Dolorosa came over to her, her handshake cordial but her old eyes merely respectful. "We're glad to have you back, Reverend Mother."

"And I'm glad to be back." She settled herself in the arbor chair that always left criss-cross ridges in you. "Tell me about yourselves."

Sister Gervaise felt the perceptible, if momentary, silence. In the years gone by they would all have burst out at once, telling about the new dalmatic that had been finished, the reply Sister Inez had given the grocer, the family things that were amusing only to them. And they would have told her about Lady, the dog. Where was Lady? Now, from their veiled expressions, it was as if they felt Reverend Mother were prying into what they had done during her absence.

"Was it hot on retreat?" Sister Gervaise asked. It was something to say.

"It's always hot in St. Louis," Mother Bernardine replied. "No worse than usual. But Father Montfort made it hot enough for us. He always lays into Superiors."

Certainly they smiled. What else could they do?

Sister Emily quivered and said out of a long blank and a determination to be charitable, "He has great devotion to Our Lady."

Through the interminable remainder of this recreation Sister Gervaise kept asking herself why they were acting this way, but her mental question was as nothing compared to Mother Bernardine's self-scrutiny. Why? What had she done? Why had she not perceived this attitude before she had gone away? Too busy, she supposed. Too taken up with the thousand cares of St. Rita's. Had it been the same? Her honesty replied that it had been but she had not bothered to notice; it had come on so gradually, and the routine had swallowed it up.

Mother Bernardine looked over at Sister Roseanne. She was the only one who had ever been guilty of anything overt. She was so young, untrained, and she was in that worst of stages for a religious: waiting to see if the Council would judge her fitted for the life or would send her back to the world. Novices at such times did strange things. You could overlook most of them. Wasn't it better to have a real woman even if she were guilty of faults, even of minor rebellions, than anemic creatures who just grubbed along? Race horses were race horses and you couldn't turn them into drays. Little Roseanne might become another Gervaise. The Superior looked at Sister Gervaise and caught her eye. Yes. There was loyalty there.

She knew, too, what had occasioned Sister Roseanne's attitude. Mother Bernardine even used the new words, "transference" and such, as they all did now. Roseanne's real worries about her chances of approval by the Council had twisted themselves into physical symptoms. Once, Reverend Mother had refused her permission to take some new pills that the doctor had not ordered. Tendency to hypochondria. Must be cured at once. For her own good. Poor thing, all that was the matter with her was that, like the rest of them, she was also tired out at the end of a heavy year. So instead of medicines there had been an Obedience of late sleeps and malted-milk eggnogs.

Certainly Mother Bernardine knew that in that case she had been right. Sister Roseanne looked flourishing enough now. But just the same a Superior could not be too careful and she must see to it that nothing really physical developed. Sometimes one accredited things to imagination, but imagination could be very real. Once, she had known a nun who had died, although the doctors all said her disease was imaginary. Too much imagination. Better err on the other side.

She had mortified herself until now. She had not even asked after Lady. No one had volunteered any information. Usually the dog would be romping around, worrying formidable and imaginary rabbits, interfering with the croquet game to the delight of everyone. They all loved Lady at St. Rita's. At least they had loved her.

Finally she asked them, "Where is Lady?"

Sister Drusilda looked embarrassed. "I should have told you," she said. "She is being disciplined. For her own good, of course."

"We knew what you would do, Reverend Mother." Sister Emily smiled.

"What was Lady up to?"

"We had to shut her up. Just for tonight, of course. If I had realized you were coming home so soon I would have had her here to greet you."

"But what did she do?"

Mother Dolorosa, who as sacristan had remote control of the greenhouse, ventured disconsolately, "She ate up my lilies."

"She likes lilies," Sister Gervaise said. "To eat, I mean. She's a very aesthetic animal. She lives on lilies. She's the lily-eating dog, straight out of Swinburne or Tennyson or some such like that."

Dear, dear, Mother Bernardine thought, you don't really need to try so hard. It's nice of you and I appreciate it, but I don't think I need that much help yet. At least I hope not.

"Then you should punish her, of course," Mother Bernardine said.

"We did. Just to teach her a lesson," Sister Drusilda explained. "Isn't that what you'd do, Reverend Mother?"

Sister Gervaise did not voice her objection, but she wanted to cry out: No. That isn't what she'd do at all—at least not in the old days. But she said nothing. The thought came involuntarily of what it would be like if Sister Drusilda, for instance, were the Superior. How would the community like that? Didn't they even see what a blessing they had?

But Reverend Mother approved. "You were absolutely right," she said, and went at once to Lady's kennel. From some distance she could hear the dog whining, straining to be with her. No. She would not loosen Lady. Could not have divided discipline in the house. They were right. Only she wished they weren't right, and she let Lady jump all over her in a perfect ecstasy of welcome. The dog's jubilation only accentuated the stiffness of the nuns.

They would be better off, Sister Gervaise knew, now that the drive for examinations was on. The classes were keener.

It was always strange how eager the students were just before exams. How much more prayerful, too.

Jeanne Collins had asked, "Sister, do you know a saint who's good for exams?"

"Good for exams?"

"You know—whom you pray to, to be sure you pass. Or maybe you know some absolutely sure prayers."

"Yes, I do."

"I knew you would!"

"Did you?"

"Oh, you know everything, Sister."

"Not quite. But I do know a prayer."

"Tell me!"

"The *Hail Mary*."

"Oh, that one! I mean, you know, something special, like a novena or some saint like St. Jude or somebody who'll be sure you pass!"

"Look, Jeanne, I'm not a witch doctor."

"Why, I don't know what you mean."

"I'm sure you don't. You want a formula, and I don't deal in spells and charms. I know some saints who are very fine people and seem to have a special interest in certain things, and I'm all for them. But what I advise you to do is to settle down and grub up on your work and say a *Hail Mary* now and then. I've always found Our Lady very helpful—*after* you've done all you can."

"Thank you, Sister." Jeanne went away. She hadn't got the point at all. If it were any other girl, she would go around saying that that Sister was crazy, but not Jeanne. She was far too docile. If she did indeed become a nun she would become another Emily. Well, there was nothing the matter with that, in a way.

Oh dear! Emily. It reminded her. She never had cleaned out Sister Emily's biology cupboard. She had used it way back in February to store make-up tins, crepe hair and an assortment of didos. It might have been all right at the time, because there had been plenty of room, but now, with the end of the school year in sight, she must get those things out of there. Sister Emily always cleaned everything up at the end, just as if she were about to be moved, ready for the Obedience that came in the summer. There wasn't much chance of Sister Emily's being moved from St. Rita's, any more than there was much chance for herself, thanks be to God. Most of the nuns would wait for their status without too much fear, although there was always a moment or two of excitement, until you saw that your name did not appear, which meant you stayed where you were.

Sister Emily alone was always ready—to do God's will, of course. She also had a right to her own cupboard in any case, and one of these days it must be cleaned out. Not that anything had been said. Sister Emily just let things go on and on like that, offering it up. Why hadn't she reminded Sister Gervaise weeks ago? Nudged her a little bit? She hadn't really meant to clutter up the cupboard so long. Well, she would have to take the things out for the graduation play anyway. Might as well stay where they were till then. Rehearsals were taking up a good deal of time just now. She had to plot out the positions for the Women of Canterbury and have what amounted to a football chalk talk for the Women tomorrow. The boys were doing pretty well.

Somehow or other she would have to get full-sized mirrors down in classroom 3-B if those girls were to get into their headgears and draperies right. That would be a mess.

And of course it would have to be Emily's classroom. Why couldn't it be Consolata's?

Here it was mid-May already and Sister Consolata had taken on a new job of training the alumnae for their May Day, which was held at the end of May now instead of the first, because of weather conditions. It was safer at the end of the month and this year should be perfect. It had been almost unseasonably warm so far.

Sister Gervaise was displeased with Sister Consolata. She should be fighting for the Cause and instead she was allowing the old girls to sing the hymns they knew—all the old chestnuts, bad music, bad words. She said they did not know any better hymns. But that was no reason to give up, was it? It would ruin the May Day and Mr. Alemando's statue.

Margaret Fleming had asked her yesterday if the model had arrived yet. It had not, as far as she knew, and they were all distressed. Suppose it did not come on time? What would they do? Have a May Day around an empty niche or, what they had always done before, put some ugly plaster thing up there to be an insult to the eye.

Margaret did not want that any more than she wanted it herself. Margaret was one girl whom she had trained to good, liturgical taste. Although to tell the truth she did did not seem to mind the old hymns and sang them with gusto.

"How are things going with you and Jim?" Sister Gervaise had asked.

"Mm—mm. You did it. We've set the date."

If she hadn't asked, would she have been told? Well, she would have heard the banns at the ten-o'clock Mass.

"When?"

"June. That's romantic enough, isn't it?"

"Romantic or not, it's good."

So there was something settled, anyway. As for the Morrisons and their problems she had had no way of knowing about them. Rosemary had settled down; Mrs. Morrison nodded to her when they met; Mr. Morrison, whom she seldom saw, looked sheepish and hurried past.

It was the very afternoon when Margaret had spoken to her that at last Mrs. Morrison's reserve had broken down. She intercepted the nun hurrying back to the convent after rehearsal, making her late for dinner.

"I understand," she said, "that you have been speaking to my husband."

"Quite some time ago, yes."

"Don't you think it's a good idea to hear both sides of a question before you make up your mind?"

"Why, yes." She wanted to say that she hadn't made up her mind, but that was not true. She had.

"And while we're on the subject, I have always thought a mother might know more about her daughter than an outsider. Do you agree with me?"

"Yes—in general."

"In general? You mean in this particular case someone else might? You, for instance?"

"I know precious little about Rosemary."

"Really? Isn't it your duty to know your pupils?"

She couldn't have it both ways! Yet somehow this, too, was unanswerable. Maybe she should have pursued Rosemary more. Yet after receiving Mr. Morrison's confidence, she found it difficult to know what to do. Apparently whatever she might have done would have been wrong.

"I can only know them if they'll let me," she said, but it sounded weak.

"We shall not bring this subject up again," Mrs. Morrison said.

"But we've got nowhere! It isn't closed!"

"It is closed as far as I am concerned. Good evening, Sister."

How could that woman manage to put you in the wrong so completely? If Mr. Morrison had wanted to make his point, he could not have illustrated it better. Yet she had not heard his wife's side of the story, and she had not taken enough time with Rosemary. That was all there was to it, and it made her feel none too good.

She was distressed, therefore, when Mother Bernardine sent for her that evening. Of all days, Sister Emily had taken that one to solicit Mother's help in getting her closet straightened out. They bumped into each other every day! Why couldn't she just have mentioned it herself?

As Mother Bernardine watched the retreating figure of Sister Gervaise, she was thinking the same thought.

Mother Bernardine had examined her conscience, trying to find if the fault lay with her for the unrest of the community. She had always been honest with herself, but in the preceding week, she thought, she had been provided with more occasions for self-examination than even those given by Father Montfort's points for meditation.

Somewhere, she knew, she had been wrong. That was the trouble with people, she had often said, when injustices were done them. They failed to look for the real thing in themselves that had been the occasion of the misunderstanding. Usually if people blamed you, even erroneously, a little examination of conscience would reveal that you were wrong somewhere. Often only their analyses would be incorrect.

Your fault would be there, although they could not diagnose it. There always was a cause within yourself if you were humble enough to ferret it out.

Mother Bernardine was humble enough. She had been giving this advice to her subjects for many years and now she took it to herself. She watched herself carefully at recreation; she measured every word of censure and of praise; she studied her own attitudes of mind and heart. She was even less attentive to Lady and positively spoiled Sister Roseanne. During these days she did nothing without consulting the Discreets.

But even their attitude troubled her. "Was I right in this?" "Yes, Mother. Yes, Mother, yes, yes, yes." Couldn't they say anything else? A dumb devil has got into them, she thought. They were supposed to advise her, not to agree.

She went to her regular confessor and he assured her that there was no sin in what she was doing, but she hadn't supposed there was any, so that didn't help much. Besides, poor man, he didn't have any chance to see her on her daily round of office.

So she spoke to the Lord and she said, "I know there's something the matter with me. I've even thought that I crave affection too much, but I really know, down underneath, that that isn't it. I've been over everything and except for the things I've done to you (but I love you just the same) I can't find anything wrong with me, so it's up to you to show me."

Then, having spoken thus familiarly, she slipped into the easy and sacred phrases, saying over and over, "Sweet Holy Ghost, illumine my mind. Light of the World, shine upon me. Seat of Wisdom, pray for me."

Her prayer was answered. Later she recognized that the

Lord had begun the answer in what she called, "the Gervaise case."

She had felt good that night, having decided that perhaps she had not been spontaneous enough of late and she had positively romped with Lady on the lawn during recreation. All the nuns joined in and it had been as close to an almost-forgotten joy as she had known.

She had even laughed when Father Fleury from the missions had caught her out, her face flushed, the dog's stick held high. The priest had not been at all angry with them for refusing to help him during the summer. He understood perfectly. He had laughed and said, "I thought I'd give it a whirl. Nothing like trying. But I really didn't think even His Excellency could get you up there. You're a stubborn lot of women." He had said it jocosely though, so it was harmless. Then he added, "Why don't you send Lady up? If I can't have you, why don't you let me have your dog?"

The nuns chorused: "Oh no!" That was good. Mother Bernardine had suspected that they resented Lady.

"Not even the dog?" Father Fleury had grimaced. "I could use her up at Warpath."

"You don't get her yet, Father. There's many a growl left in the old dog yet!"

Then they had composed themselves, and Lady, great hulk that she was, confused herself with a lapdog and tried to climb on Sister Inez's knees. Yes, it had been almost an old-fashioned evening until Sister Emily, her face drawn into its usual self-consciousness, had come to her and stammered out the purpose of her mission. Sister Gervaise, it seemed, had been using the biology cupboard since last February's play. No, she had not spoken to Sister Gervaise about it. The

Holy Rule said that no one should admonish another, so she had come directly to Mother Superior. Had she done wrong?

"No," Mother Bernardine had said. "You are perfectly right." But inside her a tiny, perverse imp was saying that it wished Sister Emily had been brave enough to have taken matters into her own hands and dumped the offending things out of her own cupboard. But she was right. One must uphold the Rule.

"I will speak to Sister Gervaise about this, of course."

"I hope you don't think I am doing wrong to come to you about this, Reverend Mother," Sister Emily reiterated.

"How could I think so?"

"I betook myself to the Blessed Sacrament," Sister Emily added.

Mother Bernardine repressed a smile. Only Sister Emily would say "betook." It was straight out of the book of rules.

"Of course you did, Sister. I'm sure you came in a spirit of charity."

There she was, talking like a book herself.

"Oh yes, Mother. I think very highly of Sister Gervaise. She works very hard. I wouldn't want you to be too severe with her."

Alert to every nuance, Mother Bernardine asked, "Severe? Do I seem to be severe? Lately, I mean?"

Maybe she had it at last. Maybe they thought she was too hard on them. Once, long ago, she remembered that she had been severe in her judgments on the postulants. She remembered saying that she couldn't understand how girls with a religious vocation could be so rude. Then she found out that they weren't rude, just frank, and remembered that she herself had had external faults, attributable to her milieu, when she had entered. She had become a religious to get rid of her faults, not because she had already got rid of them. She had changed toward others then, hadn't she? "Have I been particularly severe lately?" she asked again.

"Oh no, Reverend Mother! Oh, certainly not! I only wanted to say that I don't want you to be, I mean."

"I understand, Sister."

Sister Emily, the most perfect religious in the house—and a truly sweet woman underneath, the Superior knew—was still hesitating. Then she said, "Will you enjoin me a penance, Reverend Mother?"

"For what?"

"For any of self that may have crept in."

"Sister, dear, I don't think any has crept in. Really I don't. I think that you are absolutely right."

She should have known then what the trouble was. Or at least after she had dismissed a chastened Sister Gervaise, promising, incidentally, to get her suitable cupboards of her own, things which, she now remembered, she had promised for three years and which Sister Gervaise had not mentioned in over two. For she had been thinking, hadn't she, that Sister Gervaise had been wrong, of course, as Sister Emily had not been, but how good it was to be wrong just once in a while and to be wrong in such nice big ways as Sister Gervaise acknowledged herself to be.

Yes. In her nightly examen of conscience Sister Gervaise realized it fully. In so many ways, this year had been crowded with mistakes. Next year, God willing, would be different. She still had Theresa, and if Theresa had the quality which Sister Gervaise's father had found in her, she would devote herself to bringing it out.

For the rest, it had been through her own fault, through her fault. Well, let's not exaggerate. Not through her grievous fault. But God knows, she had been sufficiently in the wrong.

The next morning, however, she felt different about it all.

Chapter 11

ON THE FOLLOWING MORNING Sister Gervaise felt tired of always being in the wrong. There had been moments like last night's when she had determined never to fight again, but she always did.

"But Mother," she found herself remonstrating, "a dance after the play will spoil the whole effect. They're supposed to be left . . ." She dangled the sentence, cut off by the practicality of Mother Bernardine's glance and the even more practical presence of Sister Drusilda. She had wanted to say, "left feeling sublime."

They wouldn't, of course. They might as well fold up the chairs, sprinkle resin on the floor, and let the orchestra make the noises that young people seemed to enjoy.

"Now you'd better listen to me, Sister. I have no great love for those dances," Mother Bernardine answered, "but we have to work with the pastor. That's an important point. Monsignor Cooney has been bending backward for you. He's trying to reform the church music. He let you cut out the minstrel shows and give that beautiful St. Patrick's Day play instead. Then he wanted all the girls to be in the senior drama—it brings in the parents—but he let you go on with this 'Murder' thing."

"*Murder in the Cathedral,* Mother. It's about a saint."

"I know. But how many are in the cast?"

"Twelve, Mother, including the verse choir."

"That's what I mean. Parents, a few friends and about thirty disgruntled seniors who didn't get a part. So he is allowing the girls to run a dance afterward. At least that will give you an audience."

She didn't want an audience like that. Gigglers who were restive until the chairs were moved. Half of them would come shuffling in during the second act on those special wooden shoes she was sure they invented for latecomers, armed with the crinkly candy bags that the enemies of the drama supplied.

Now Mother Bernardine was not a martinet. She was a very reasonable woman, even if she always did make Sister Gervaise feel in the wrong when she was really on the right side and fighting for the Cause. The Superior would not object at all if Sister Gervaise stated her case. Only now there did not seem to be any case. They needed money for central heating; to raise money you had to have an audience; to get an audience you had to have a dance; Q.E.D., just like that.

"All right, Reverend Mother. We'll have the dance."

Mother Bernardine was kind enough to say nothing after such a submission but from the corner where Sister Drusilda was perpetually filing receipted bills Sister Gervaise was sure she heard a grunt of satisfaction.

Being the bursar, Sister Drusilda almost professionally disapproved of anything arty. She had bills to pay which she managed very well, and saw no sense in all this falderal. If she had any weakness it was for the good old hymns, and she admitted that this new Gregorian music sounded to her like a funeral. Now they wanted to cut out "Here Comes the Bride." You might just as well not get married in church at all. Wait till Margaret Fleming and her mother heard about that. Just before the wedding, too!

Sister Drusilda had not intended to intrude but her cough (which had been misinterpreted as a grunt) must have attracted the attention of Sister Gervaise, because she looked over as if she were going to speak. But something stopped her.

"Oh!" she exclaimed.

It had come at last. Maybe it had been here a long time and nobody had told her. But there it was! Her eye had fallen on the model of the statue.

Actually it had been here some time, but neither Mother Bernardine nor Sister Drusilda would let anybody see it. That terrible model! It would have to be changed. They had agreed, from the moment when Felix Alemando full of worship for his own work had uncrated it, that it would never go up in any niche here. Not the way it was. Not even if the alumnae insisted with one voice. Which they wouldn't. Not when they saw it. And this was supposed to be Our Lady.

"He's done it!" Sister Gervaise cried. "It's beautiful!"

Mother Bernardine rose and Sister Drusilda gave up her filing. They frankly stared at the statue, at each other, back at the statue, in what Sister Gervaise would have called a "double take." This is what they saw:

A gaunt figurine of a hollow-faced woman of incredible length whose feet weren't finished but stuck—yes—*into* a pockmarked spheroid, her height accentuated by a twist of veil that formed a conical hood. And worst of all, the hands, which were large with overdeveloped knuckles, were all out of proportion to the rest.

148 ✒

"Arthritis," Sister Drusilda had said of them, laughing.

Now Mother Bernardine was the first to speak. "You can't mean that." Her tone conveyed that she had put up with a great deal, but this was altogether too much.

"But I do. I do mean it."

A moment had come to Sister Gervaise such as comes only to artists. You could not tell anyone else about it because no one would understand. It was recompense for all the times you had to put up with being thought eccentric, even a little touched. It was the sudden splendor of perfection.

"Oh yes," she said, "yes, yes, yes!"

If she had fallen into a mystic trance the way poor Margaret Mary used to under the butternut tree, her two Sisters could not have been more perplexed. All that the Superior could do was to say, "Now, really!"

As if that had shattered the statue, Sister Gervaise's moment perished. She could not recapture it herself. How could she explain it to others?

Mother Bernardine had been talking to her. "Are you listening, Sister?"

"Yes, Mother."

"I was saying that Mr. Alemando was quite reasonable about it—for an artist. He'll cut down the height and make the feet appear. He won't put roses on the feet, although we asked him to. And, of course, he'll change those awful hands. I'd like to persuade him to have Our Lady carry a rosary. Don't you think that would be better?"

Sister Gervaise made no reply at all. She couldn't. Why not have Our Lady *say* the rosary? How would that be? Sister Drusilda said, "Of course the way it is, it's all out of proportion."

Proportion? Sister Gervaise remembered the Christmas crib and the huge Infant, whose size measured somewhere between that of the sheep and the ox. But that was all right. They were used to that.

Mother Bernardine stopped the bursar with a glance. "I think we had better sit down and discuss what Sister Gervaise sees that's attractive about this—this statue."

She was being fair. Working hard at it. It was incredible that anyone could admire this monstrosity, but if there were anything to be said for it she would listen and be as gentle as possible in her correction of the wayward viewpoint of this strange daughter of hers.

It was the kind of tolerance that, years ago, would have infuriated Sister Gervaise, but to which she had so accustomed herself that all that happened now was a kind of limp feeling. She was used to it. Even her best friend, Sister Consolata, defended her by saying that she was better since she had got rid of a lot of those arty notions—which meant, since she had learned to keep still. Now she had to say something. She would try the indirect approach.

"Don't you think Mr. Alemando is a good artist?"

"I've always heard he was."

"Maybe he's great. Maybe a great artist would know more about what is beautiful than we would." Was she being too bold?

"I can still see," Mother Bernardine replied. "What's beautiful about that thing?"

This was getting difficult. It would be like trying to explain a sunset or a sea. Those things just are. You don't explain them. And then, Mother Bernardine was noted for her good taste. Everybody said the way she had had the old wing of the convent redecorated when she first came here was lovely and, in a very usual sort of way, it was. There was nothing offensively ugly about it.

Yet the Superior's tone was maternal enough and encouraging. "Tell us, Sister. I really want to know."

Under obedience Sister Gervaise attempted the impossible. For what she had seen was this:

A form of a woman, graceful and slender as a lily, rising spontaneously like a flower out of a bulb, but a bulb that was the moon, the real moon, a barren planet, and from it the white, tapering fecundity of the woman; the shadowed features, like the dark madonnas of the icons, beyond mere attraction of the eyes, soaring over conscious prettiness into a sublimity of conquered pain, surrounded by a floating veil that lifted like a halo, but more, like the chalice of a lily. Above all were the hands. These were not the plump, dimpled hands of the self-indulgent. They were toil worn from many years. They were the hands of suffering, twisted as were the tortured hands of Christ, knotted by hard years, but the hands of a mother, tender on the heads of little children.

She said all that. For a moment Mother Bernardine seemed to see it, but when she looked again at the model she shook her head regretfully, as if what she tried to discover simply wasn't there.

"My dear Sister," she said, "I think that's all very lovely. I'm glad you find that in it, and I'm sure Mr. Alemando meant all that. But Christian art is for the people. How many do you suppose would understand it?" She turned to the bursar. "Sister Drusilda, what do you think?"

Sister Drusilda made a wry face. "I think it isn't devotional." She went back to her filing.

Then Mother Bernardine, intending to be considerate,

said all the wrong things. She gave Sister Gervaise a homily on the purpose of church art, how it was to foster piety, make people lift their hearts and minds to God, all the things with which Sister Gervaise thoroughly agreed.

That was it. Always putting her in the wrong, she thought. She walked the length of the corridor where the foundresses frowned at her from their portraits, down the stairs and out beneath the empty niche where the statue was to stand. Always making it seem as if she favored art with a capital A over piety and devotion and prayer and all good things.

Must God always be worshiped by tawdriness? Were meretricious things that begot sentimentality the only things pleasing to the Most High? Weren't the girls being educated out of that sort of cheapness in the classroom, and then ruined outside by pink plaster angels?

She wasn't being fair and she knew it, because things were not that bad here. There were no candy-cake cherubs. But everything was a compromise.

Not devotional indeed, she thought. I suppose it's devotional to have a dance after *Murder in the Cathedral*. I suppose it helps piety to have had the Lohengrin wedding march played in church all these years. Well, thank God, they'd got rid of that.

By the time she was halfway to the convent, she was thoroughly aroused, and, instead of being tempted to give it all up, she was beginning to see it as a crusade. In the past, she had been bothered by temptations to think that she was disobedient in not bending her will and judgment to the voice of superiors, but her confessor had straightened her out on that, and besides, Mother Bernardine had asked for her opinion. She had given it. A lot of good it had done!

In the Superior's office, Mother Bernardine said, "Well, you can't tell me I handled that very well."

Sister Drusilda filed another bill. "What else could you do?" Her gesture put Sister Gervaise and all modern art in its proper pigeonhole. "You can't have her going around singing the praises of things like that."

"No." The monosyllable was a drawl. "But I was aggravated by this, coming on top of last night's things. I let it show. Do I do that often?"

"Indeed you don't. Too little, for my thinking."

"Look. You can speak frankly to me—at least you. We both know what we're facing." A glance of understanding passed between the two women. "Tell me frankly, what's the matter with me?"

"Nothing, Reverend Mother. Nothing, really."

That "really" there. Was that the clue?

"Look now. When I first came here, I think I was a little too lenient. I conquered that. But I don't think you can say I am a Simon Legree even now, can you?"

"Certainly not."

"Then what's the matter with the community?"

"I haven't noticed anything—much."

"What have you noticed, then?"

"They seem tense, that's all."

"I know. What have I done wrong? You have an obligation to tell me. Particularly now."

"I don't know, Mother. I wish I did, but I don't. I've been thinking about it since Easter. Maybe it's the end of the season; they'll be all right once the summer comes. They always are."

"No. They'll just cover it over with distractions, the way I did before I went on retreat. That won't help." She paused, looking for an abstracted moment at the Madonna. "I've been over everything. You don't think it was the refusal I gave the Bishop, do you?"

"No," Sister Drusilda said slowly. "I know it isn't that. Even Father Fleury understood. The Sisters couldn't have taken it, even if some thought they could."

"I've thought of everything. Even the dog. But that's too silly."

"What about the dog?"

"Do I seem to treat Lady as if she were my own?"

Sister Drusilda laughed her dry laugh. "What ever made you think that?"

"I've thought of everything."

"I guess you have."

"And I can't find anything really wrong. That's the trouble. I've been squeezing my conscience dry and I can't recall a single thing. Except sometimes with Sister Gervaise —but she's so strong and I'm so confident of her loyalty. You know, it's even a relief to think that maybe I overdid it a bit with her. Didn't I?"

They looked over at Mr. Alemando's madonna. Then, after contemplating it a while, Mother Bernardine shook her head. "No," she said, still looking at it, "I don't think I did."

Wrapped in her own thoughts, Sister Gervaise had paid scant attention to the lean figure of a man who walked slowly down the path ahead of her. Not until she excused herself, in order to pass, did she recognize Mr. Alemando.

His mouth smiled at her but his eyes had the hurt look of a bewildered spaniel. They needed no preliminaries.

"I've heard the verdict. What are you going to do?" she asked.

"I go into the chapel and pray."

I'm not, she thought. I'm going to fight this. She flashed him her best smile, showing she was on his side. "Pray for courage," she called back, and proceeded to her cell.

Now what to do? There was one way. Mother Bernardine had to be convinced of the rightness of the statue. The alumnae were presenting it. She would rally them, get the ones who had been her drama students and those who had been in Sister Consolata's art class and a few of the music-club girls. Let them talk up the devotional aspects of Alemando's madonna. They could convince Mother Bernardine that somebody besides herself could find beauty there, and that she wasn't totally a freak. No. That mustn't be her motive. Too personal. The motive was the external glory of God.

The first one she would call would be Margaret Fleming. That girl had good taste. And her coming marriage would mean showers at which she could drop a few hints to the other girls.

She leafed through her file index and found the Fleming number. It was with determination that she dialed from the wall phone in the hall. Once she heard someone stirring down at the end of the corridor. She didn't care who heard her. She was no coward. Besides, she was right.

She got Margaret at once and was gratified with the response.

"Of course I'll plug your statue, Sister. If you say it's beautiful, I say it's beautiful." Then a conspiratorial tone entered. "But will you do something for me?"

"Depends on what it is."

"I'm just brokenhearted. You know, they tell me I can't

have 'Here Comes the Bride' at my wedding. Please, Sister! Talk to Monsignor Cooney for me. He'll do anything you say. Just this once? I wouldn't feel married without it."

There was a prolonged silence from Sister Gervaise.

"Won't you please, Sister?"

"Margaret, it isn't only the Monsignor. The Bishop doesn't want it." In her mind she added, "Or the Pope. Or the Holy Ghost."

"Just for me, Sister? They haven't read out that letter from the Bishop yet. Tell them to hold off for just a little while. Won't you?"

"Do you know what music means?"

"Means?" Her voice was vague. "I don't get it. What does it mean?"

"Music does mean something. Honestly. But as long as you don't know, I don't suppose it matters."

"Thank you, Sister! I knew you'd find a way out. Thanks again."

"Margaret! Margaret!" But the phone was dead. What did the girl think she had said?

Back to her cell for another try. Perhaps it would be as well to make out a list. She started to do it, penciling out the hopeless ones, putting question marks after the doubtful ones. When she had finished, she reviewed the names.

It was true. There was not the name of a truly pious girl left. There were bright girls, thoroughly good girls, but most of them had been branded at school as either sophisticates or a trifle touched. Radicals, like the clergy who took an interest in the liturgy; like people who worked in Harlem; like nuns who disapproved of minstrel shows and put on plays by T. S. Eliot.

What kind of Cause was this anyway, she was thinking,

156 ✍

when a knock came at the door and her answer entered in the person of Sister Drusilda. She had a book under her arm.

"I was going by. I thought you might like this. It will give you an idea of how Mother and I feel."

There she goes again, ranging herself on the side of authority.

"Thank you, Sister. I'll be glad to read it."

The page was marked but she knew the story of old. It was about an aged monk who had charge of the Christmas crib and had loved and tended it for years. A new abbot, however, replaced the beloved figures with a new set, very chaste and very cold. Out of devotion, the old monk had taken the discarded Infant to his cell.

Christmas Eve it was noticeable that only the curious came and went, praised and appraised the crib as a work of art but did not pray. So at night, moved by a holy impulse, the monk went to the crib and exchanged infants.

The next day the faithful came and knelt with eyes only for the Babe. And the abbot, who was a good man at heart, saw the devotion and was moved by it. Instead of reproving the monk, he himself carried the sheep and the shepherds and Our Lady down from the attic, and the newer figures were never seen again.

"And happily, the old monk knelt there that evening. The glow of the Christmas lights fell upon him. Softly, from the organ, came the tones of the '*Adeste fideles*,' while from the church echoed the whispered prayers of many devout people. A feeling of deep peace . . ."

Nonsense. The abbot had been right in the first place and the old monk guilty of rank disobedience in forcing his Superior's hand.

At the thought Sister Gervaise looked down guiltily at the

list of supporters she had drawn up. Why did things have to get so complicated? Forcing the Superior's hand? If it were wrong for the monk, it was wrong for her. She tore up the list.

She would take her Cause to Our Lady. She went down to chapel and started her novena at once.

Chapter 12

Iᴛ ᴡᴏᴜʟᴅ have been a neat solution if her prayers had been answered on the ninth day of her novena, as they are in stories, but she had scarcely started when the Pope came to her support and she had to turn the remaining days into thanksgiving. She read the encyclical on church art over and over again. Yes. Church art, like music, must be prayer. No exaggerations, no merely secular intrusions. It must be significant and Catholic. Above all, there was a masterly condemnation of the tawdry art objects that had cluttered sanctuaries for so many years of pietism and bad taste. Good. Armed with this, she could take up the cudgels for God and Mr. Alemando.

She had been certain that it was a direct answer to prayer until she had to wait outside Mother Superior's door. Sometimes, it seemed to her, that vast portions of her religious life had been spent waiting in corridors like this while she cast little prayers toward the Sacred Heart whose statue stood at the end of the hall. She made an involuntary examination of conscience in preparation for the scrutiny of Reverend Mother; prepared answers for everything except what she would be called to account for; and, finally, her hand wet with nervousness, fumbled for the doorknob.

Why did she have to be like this? She wasn't a novice.

She was a mature woman armed with a papal encyclical and about to state an objective case. She was going to have the dance after the play, wasn't she? And she hadn't really bothered Monsignor Cooney for a long time.

At least Mother Bernardine was alone. She looked up and exclaimed, "Oh! Isn't it funny? I was just going to send for you." She was not very formidable today. "Sit down," she added. "I've something for you."

From the perfect order of her desk drawer she whisked out a pamphlet. It was an identical copy of the encyclical Sister Gervaise clutched in her damp hand.

"There." Mother Bernardine smiled. "Now that we have Rome speaking, I hope we'll settle all this once and for all. I want you to read this, Sister."

She couldn't very well reply that she had practically memorized it and had it with her, or was trying to force it on Mother Bernardine. All she could do was to accept it, hoping the Superior would not notice how clumsily she attempted to conceal her own copy.

"There. The Pope has some wonderful things to say about all this modern art of yours," Mother Bernardine continued. "He thinks it's pretty pagan. Personally, I think the Communists are in back of it. But I'm sure this will straighten you out once you've read it."

"But the Pope doesn't condemn modern art, does he? I thought . . ."

"Oh, you've read it? That's good. No, just those grotesque things like that awful madonna you liked so well."

"Mr. Alemando isn't a Communist, Mother."

"I don't suppose so. But one gets infected without realizing what's happening. They're awfully clever, you know. I suppose half the poor artists haven't the least idea what they're doing, with all their meaningless lines and the two eyes in the middle of the profile. Even poor Mr. Alemando makes Our Lady with no feet!" She was warming to her subject, falling into the familiar pitfall of implying that all artists were naïve, dupes, frauds or completely mad, poor things, and that, after all, the only safe ones were dead ones.

"Why," she proceeded, "the other day I saw a picture by a famous man and he had drawn Our Lady with a big hole right in the middle of her. You don't approve of such nonsense, do you, Sister?"

From some inner resource of courage Sister Gervaise managed to say, "Yes, Mother." She had seen the reproduction and had rejoiced that a former pagan had been inspired to turn his great skill to something tremendously significant.

"Well. Well, indeed." Mother Superior seemed incapable of saying any more. Her brow was puckered with worry as if she had detected some unfathomable depth of soul in one of her subjects, which she was patiently resolved, at whatever cost, to penetrate.

There was nothing left to do. Holding both copies of the encyclical close to her, Sister Gervaise rose. "I'll study this carefully."

"I forgot something, Sister. I must speak of it. I don't believe it's so, but I heard you were organizing the alumnae to achieve your own will. Naturally, I know it can't be so."

Involuntarily Sister Gervaise looked over at the empty corner where Sister Drusilda's files stood. It was she who had come to her room, wasn't it? Who had heard her at the telephone? A wave of indignation swept over her, but she suppressed it and offered up the indignity of the betrayal for the poor souls. She said, "I did, Mother. I called up one girl."

"That was one too many."

"I know."

"I'm glad you realize it. Would you make a visit to the chapel and say three *Hail Marys*?"

Sister Gervaise walked across the campus on a wave of shame. Now she was really on the wrong side. Maybe others were right about artists. You got thinking about one thing and it swept you away and nothing else seemed to matter. You tried to be just like everybody else so that nobody would say you were odd, and then you did something stupid like calling up Margaret.

Sister Gervaise said her three *Hail Marys* with complete penitence. It was probably the realization of her imperfections that made her so gracious to the Monsignor about the dance after the play. She offered up that, too, although the dance turned out to be all the horror she had anticipated.

The play itself was satisfactory. That was the best that could be said for it. When (now that she was living in a glass house) she was trying not to throw stones, she always referred to such a performance as "interesting." It did not compromise the truth and it was perfectly safe. You could be interested in a bad thing, in just trying to see what made it so bad. Not that *Murder in the Cathedral* was a bad production; it was much worse—it was dull.

How could that be? To make *Murder* dull was as much of a feat as to make *Julius Caesar* dull. The gorgeous words flowed on, the tremendous rise was there, the wonderful significance. Joe Maguire had fine moments as the Archbishop; Nick Collasanto was an exquisitely evil Tempter.

Rosemary outdid herself as the leader of the Women of Canterbury.

Theresa, of course, not being a senior, was not eligible for the play. Well? Was that the reason? She thought it well might be. Her father was almost infallible in his judgments of actors, and if he said Theresa had it, he almost certainly must be right. And the dullness of *Murder* was perhaps the proof. Too bad Theresa wasn't better looking.

Right after the play she did what was customary. As soon as she had congratulated the actors, she hunted Theresa down to where she and her mother were busily re-sorting properties. Mrs. Doyle by this time had so merged herself into the background of the Dramatic Club that she practically blended into the scenery. It did not matter that she was there.

"Theresa!" Sister Gervaise called. "Next year is yours!"

"Mine? You mean mine?" All the students knew the formula, were waiting for the announcement. Theresa knew what it meant.

"Yes, you're It. We'll get busy so you can study over the summer."

Theresa waited for the next words. She remembered the tradition. Last year had been a boy's play and Joe Maguire had been It. Not that he had chosen *Murder in the Cathedral,* but he had been allowed to make a suggestion at least. All the leads could do that. The question came.

"Is there anything you'd particularly like to do?"

"Yes, Sister."

"Good. What?"

"Romeo and Juliet."

Oh no! And there was the smiling and approving face of Mrs. Doyle. How could Theresa get such notions? Like

163

the three-hundred-pound girl who wanted to be a ballet dancer. A buck-toothed Juliet! It was the same thing. Couldn't they even look at themselves in a mirror?

"I'm sorry. You see, I talked myself into doing this thing tonight. I insisted on it."

Mrs. Doyle said laughingly, "They all thought it was going to be a murder mystery."

Yes. They had. Sister Gervaise's mind was illuminated with a sudden flash. I did it defiantly; I forced it down their throats; I got hoist by my own petard; it was way over their heads. Never again.

"And it was, well, a little too ambitious. We can't take a chance like that again, can we?"

Mrs. Doyle, as usual, rallied to the nun's side. Such a relief to have parents old-fashioned enough to be on the side of authority. So rare!

"I told Theresa that, didn't I, dear? I think it was a lovely play, but all those thees and thous and things, the same like in Shakespeare. It's too much even for television. Better let Sister pick out a play for you, Terry."

"I just thought . . . you can dream, can't you, Sister?"

"Never stop. Maybe when you get to college. Sister Lourdes at the Cliffs has a wonderful drama group. She does magnificent Shakespeare. Even Charlie Costello says so, and he knows. Why, she even brought the *Taming of the Shrew* down to Loras last year, and you know how Father Schroeder is about such things. But perhaps we'd better pull in our horns a bit here. You come around to the convent tomorrow and we'll read a play together."

Yes. Tomorrow would be all right. The chairs were being folded now. When you had a dance, all that work was . . . She could repeat that formula by heart.

"What's the name of it?"

"*Mrs. MacThing.* She's a witch."

"Type casting!" Mrs. Doyle laughed, viewing her darling. She had no delusions about her offspring's personal beauty.

You've hit the nail on the head, lady, Sister Gervaise thought. She said: "It's a really nice part. Lots of sides."

"Is it juicy?"

"Fairly drips."

"Wait till I get my teeth into it!" Theresa laughed, too, not with any embarrassment, because Theresa didn't have any delusions left about herself either. Not since she had been a saint.

Mrs. Doyle was ready to go back to work. Sister Gervaise squeezed her hand.

"You're a brick," she whispered.

"You're not so bad yourself."

Then Theresa said, looking like a bowl of fudge, "Wasn't Joe Maguire *super?*"

"Super-duper. Still carrying the torch?"

"It's the love of my life!"

The tone of voice. Not the words, surely. The slight irony under them. Wasn't that funny? This was the first adult intonation Sister Gervaise had heard from Theresa. Suddenly she had grown up. Wasn't it too bad? Too bad.

The orchestra had begun to blat its noises, making hideous the night air.

"To next year," Sister Gervaise cried, over the cacophony.

"Next year!"

Unfortunately she had to stay to the bitter end in order to count the veils of the Women of Canterbury and sort out the costumes of the Tempters, so she could hear the noises that the orchestra made. It sounded to her as if it had been imported from darkest Africa. How could people stand the barbarity of these hideous screeches? Couldn't they detect the insidiousness of the rhythms? The dance was supposed to be the perfection of movement and music the perfection of sound. But this, on both counts, was the triumph of ugliness. Couldn't they tell that it was evil?

No. They couldn't.

She knew that young people did not hear the music or have any thought about the significance of their gyrations. The orchestra, to them, simply pounded out a series of rhythms, to which they got a certain amount of exercise. They were immune. Look at their faces and you would know they were all right. Constant familiarity had deadened their senses and made them deaf to the meaning of sound.

She herself had succumbed.

Once, long ago, she had been disturbed, whenever she heard it, by the caterwaulings of the juke boxes in the cafeteria; now she could sit there prefecting and not even hear them. At first she had been unable to look at the red and green stations of the cross in the convent chapel. Now they did not bother her at all. She might even get to like them. Watch out! That would never do.

Since the play had been devotional the Sisters had been allowed to attend and, although they had returned to the convent immediately after it was over, Mother Bernardine knew that all of them were still stirring. It was after eleven, but she had allowed them a late sleep, until six, tomorrow. Heaven knew when Sister Gervaise would get in.

The dance had begun. She shuddered. In the winter you could shut your window and bar out the sounds, but on a soft May night you had your choice of smothering or of being tortured by these awful noises.

She could never accustom herself to them. Others, she knew, could shut them out and apparently not be bothered by them. But she could never train herself to do this. Not in all the years of trying. Whenever the monsignor wanted a dance, she knew what she would have to go through

It was her secret. No one would ever know. They would think, like Sister Gervaise, that she wanted these dances, who had been sure of that, she knew, when all she had been doing was demanding that the pastor's wishes be followed. Sister Gervaise was under the impression that her Superior did not understand her objections.

Not understand? She understood only too well. But it was, after all, only a little mortification that both of them could well endure. Father Cooney—Monsignor—asked very little of them.

Once she thought she heard a loud noise downstairs but she could not be sure. The blaring rhythm drowned out everything, and in any case it probably would only be the door to the basement slamming. One of the Sisters going down there to take her things out of the presses in the cellar. Too bad they had to do that, but there was no room upstairs in their quarters.

Maybe, she thought, if I really listen to these noises they call music, try to analyze them, I might do better. Not want to throw my head back and howl like a dog. There were, she had been told, really scientific studies of this new jazz rhythm and people were taking it seriously. But no. It had no imagination. Its progressions were all wrong. And the tonal quality of that brass! Ugliness, that is what it was. Ugliness. Had the world turned back to ugliness? Were they decaying into primitives, going back into some dismal swamp? Offenses to the eye and ear, all about, and even good women like Gervaise, who could appreciate such things as this play tonight, though it had been an unfortunate choice, really, could be deluded by the new atrocities.

Well, she had better forget all about this, put it completely out of her mind, particularly from now on. She would never need it again. Funny how God worked. Some people's talents He used, as He was using Sister Gervaise's. Some talents, like her own, He asked to have folded up in a napkin and buried in a field. That wasn't what the parable advised, was it?

How long ago? How many years ago? In her mind's eye she could see her violin, the strings slack, then finally broken. Never played it again. Never would again. And the memories that people had had, when first she entered religion, had gradually died away so that less and less often had she been asked, "Didn't you used to play the violin?" At community fiestas they had long ago asked her to fiddle for them. She had always refused. Now they had forgotten.

Yes. She had played the violin. She could still remember the joy, the exhilaration, the wonderful nights when she had brought real beauty to the world. She had played in the Chicago Symphony Orchestra. It was, they told her, a great accomplishment for so young a girl.

Then, when she was leaving to enter the convent, her teacher had said, "Never admit you know anything about it. Music and the religious life don't mix."

She had been amazed. "I thought it would be very useful."

"No. You are an artist. That is different. If you just fiddled —well, it wouldn't matter how badly you played. But an artist can't do two things. You should practice seven, eight, fourteen hours a day. You won't be able to do that. You want to be a full-time nun, don't you?"

"Of course—but . . ."

"There are no buts. Some religious can degenerate into amateurs. You couldn't. The rest—they're not quite musicians and not quite nuns. They're torn. I have seen them. So will you. You have made a choice so from now on you will know nothing about music."

She had made the choice. She was no longer an artist, just a nun. Fully. It had left her free for all Obediences. Until now, when Sister Gervaise thought she was a Philistine.

Maybe she was, after all these years. Couldn't you lose everything? Or sacrifice everything? And again, there was no reason why a musician should have good taste in the other arts: architecture, sculpture. She might be wrong about Mr. Alemando's statue. Conceivably. Yet remembering it, how could she be? Oh dear, if she were only a thoroughly practical person like Sister Drusilda. If only she knew utterly nothing about any of the arts and could just be satisfied with liking what she liked, the way other people did.

Good. Her reminiscences had at last distracted her from ten terrifying minutes of the dance band. She was startled back to reality by an unprecedented knocking on her door.

Sister Consolata burst in without waiting to be admitted. Reverend Mother felt odd, sitting there in her little white cap, and reached hurriedly over for her veil.

"Mother! Please come! Sister Inez is at the bottom of the cellar stairs moaning something dreadful, and Lady is standing watch over her and won't let me near her."

Together they went to the cellar below the chapel where Sister Inez was lying. At Mother Bernardine's voice the dog gave up its vigil. Obedience. The dog knew the Superior.

Sister Inez was badly bruised, badly shaken, and probably had had a moment's unconsciousness from concussion. Together Sister Consolata and Mother Bernardine managed to support her to the service elevator and convey her upstairs to the infirmary.

"What happened? Can you tell me?"

"That ah-nee-mahl."

"That what? Oh yes. Animal. I see. What did Lady do?"

It seemed highly improbable but it really had been so. Lady had leaped for some faded lilies that Sister Inez was helpfully bringing down to the basement, on her way to her own clothes press. What had happened, as Mother Bernardine pieced it together, was that when Sister Inez held the lilies high, Lady had thought them a new thing to retrieve. Besides, she liked lilies. Then the full weight of the dog's body had knocked Sister Inez down the flight of stairs, bruising her badly. As a last iniquity, the animal, as she kept calling it, kissed Sister Inez's face over and over again and stood guard above her, growling, when Sister Consolata would have rushed to her assistance.

"Kees my face! That ah-nee-mahl!" Sister Inez shuddered at the recollection.

Mother Bernardine did not hesitate. She did not go to the chapel to weigh her decision before the Lord. Certainly she did not go to the kitchen because she was afraid that her resolution would perish before the piteous eyes of the dog.

She went directly to the telephone. They would still be up at the rectory; the clergy always got together for a smoke and a good-night talk after these plays. Father Fleury was in town and would be there.

She reached him only after two other voices had answered first—which was quite good. He was leaving in the morning. He would be glad to take Lady with him to Warpath. Certainly. He could put her in the car tomorrow and be off with her right after Mass. Thank you. Do you really mean it?

"Yes, Father, I mean it. Lady must go."

She hung up the receiver, determined, and back in her cell with the lights out she spent the rest of the time, until Sister Gervaise's return, mulling over in her mind what she would say to the community tomorrow.

"Sisters, Lady is gone. I have sent her to a good home with a kind priest whom you know. Last night we had a most unfortunate occurrence and though I know that no lasting harm will come of it, it was serious enough to bring me to this decision . . ."

From across the playground they were announcing that there was something the matter with "this old house." The young people were singing it, and it was repetitively clear that this old house had seen better days.

"I feel, too, and I speak for myself, that we were too much attached to Lady. Sometimes we are in danger of attaching ourselves to the symbolic values of things, inanimate objects and, certainly, to pets. They represent, perhaps, the warmth and affection we should find in each other, here in this blessed community. . . ."

She wished that this old house would fall down and get it over with.

"Sometimes, too, we are asked to give up things, even good and useful things, in which we can see no harm, in order that a greater good may be produced. It is quite clear that Lady was unaware of doing any harm. And I think—I think—sometimes we can do the greatest harm when we are unaware of it, even when we think we are doing good, can find no fault in ourselves. For Lady—Lady was proud of what she had done."

If she heard about this old house once more! At any rate, the tune would be going round and round in her head all night.

She had composed her speech completely. Then she knew that it would be far too complicated, even insolent. The nuns knew as much or more about spiritual motivations than she did. Who was she to instruct them thus?

She decided that she would make a simple statement at lunch next day. "I have sent Lady away. I think, Sisters, that you know why and I hope it's for the best."

That is precisely what she did say.

Chapter 13

IN THE REMAINING DAYS before their late May Day, when the statue was to be unveiled, Sister Gervaise could remember only one moment of consolation. There never could be open hostility at St. Rita's, but now there was not merely tension, but positive disapproval of the Superior. It made it doubly hard for Sister Gervaise, who had her own personal reason for dissatisfaction, to be loyal.

Yet what had Mother done? She had got rid of a pet of the convent who had proved too big for them to handle, and whom, after all, she had loved more than they had. If she had punished them, she had punished herself worse. And there was no great issue involved in that. The great issue was the statue.

Her moment of consolation had come when she was putting some props back in the attic, being particularly careful now, since the affair of the cupboard. In fact, the only thing remaining in Sister Emily's domain were the wall mirrors she had finally got Mr. MacGill to put up, and which he was in no hurry to take down.

In the attic, curiously, she had lifted up a moth-eaten drape. Under it were two twisted, brass candelabra, contorted with wheat sheaves and bunched grapes, sprouting innumerable lotus leaves that miraculously supported the remainders of colored vigil lights. In back was a tipsy and sickening statue of some forgotten saint, with the worst of its peaches-and-cream complexion mercifully flecking off.

Yes. She remembered when these things had desecrated the sanctuary. She even remembered when she had grown used to them, as everybody else had. But now, no remorseful abbot would climb up here to retrieve them. They were done for, disintegrating in the corruption of their own bad taste. Yes. Ugliness destroyed itself. And things were better, certainly, than they had been back in those days.

Yet, she thought, as she buried them again, maybe people had really been able to pray better in their time because of them. If so, they had served a purpose.

See, she complimented herself, I really do have a proper sense of values. Who says I don't put devotion first?

She was holding on to that thought grimly as the alumnae May Day procession, singing "Bring Flowers of the Rarest," came from the chapel toward the unveiling of the statue. Deliberately, heroically, no matter what happened, she was putting devotion first.

Felix Alemando stood at the edge of the crowd. She wondered what he had done, what he was thinking of now? His spaniel eyes always looked sad anyway, so you couldn't tell. He suffered, always. Mother Bernardine was calm and unruffled. Sister Drusilda wore an expression of pious consolation. You couldn't tell what to expect.

As Margaret Fleming passed (slighting the word "Queen" and stressing every "of" in the hymn in a Bing Crosbyish sort of way—"Queen *of* the angels, Queen *of* the May"), she gave Sister Gervaise an understanding and distracting sidelong glance. Maybe things would be all right after all.

174 ☞

The girls formed a semicircle around the veiled statue. It was really very pretty, charming, a picture of youth and dedication, the flowers fresh along their arms, maidens coming to the ancient rite of tribute to the Virgin of Virgins. The president of the alumnae stepped forward. There was a moment's difficulty with the string but not enough to destroy the effect. Then the statue was revealed.

Mr. Alemando had betrayed her.

The hood was pushed back; the face was "idealized"; the hands were softened; the feet were delineated so that the Lady did not rise from the moon bulb but pressed it down; and worst of all—oh, you can't have done this to me—there were roses on each instep!

Nor was this as bad as the fact that nothing had been changed fully. The figure was still long and the hands large. The face was not conventionally pretty; it just wasn't significant. The whole thing should have had a name card on it: Compromise.

The nun looked over at Sister Drusilda and read the message in her eyes.

"I don't like it very much, but at least I don't dislike it as much as before."

The ceremony went on, and it was a relief when the floral crown was placed, only slightly askew, atop the head of the Virgin. It didn't matter. The group could break up now.

Margaret Fleming whispered to her, "Why, Sister, I don't see what all the fuss was about. Honestly, it isn't half as bad as I expected."

What had she expected?

As soon as she could, Sister Gervaise, avoiding Mother

Bernardine, went bravely over and ranged herself beside Mr. Alemando. She looked at him accusingly.

"I'm sorry for you," she said. "But you shouldn't have done it."

"No?" His moist eyes were smiling at her. "But I think I should."

"Why?"

"Obedience is better than beauty."

Again! Must they always say things like that? Even Felix Alemando?

"You compromised," she replied firmly. "That's the greatest sin."

He was patient with her. "You are wrong, little Sister. We are pioneers. We press on too fast. The Reverend Mother is the right one. We must lead the people, as the Holy Father leads them—not so far ahead that they cannot see us. You and I, we see the vision. Slowly we unfold it to them. Already we have come a long way."

She remembered the attic. "I know."

"Do you also know what I would call this statue?"

Contritely she remembered what she had called it in her mind a few moments ago. She would not say that.

"What would you call it?"

"The Madonna of the Transition."

She looked at it again. Seeing it in a different light, it was not so bad. Heavens! Here she was thinking exactly what she had condemned earlier. Not so bad, indeed.

Mr. Alemando was going on, almost as if to himself. "God has called me to live in this in-between age. That is my vocation. This is my time. I will make the sacrifice to the will of God."

Then, spontaneously, Sister Gervaise said what she would never dream of saying had she not been so deeply moved. "Mr. Alemando," she said, "I knew you were a great artist. Now I know you are a great man."

She turned away abruptly and went closer to the statue. Mother Bernardine came and stood beside her, looking up critically.

"Well," she said, "that's better."

Sister Gervaise said, "Yes, Mother, it's better," not meaning the same thing at all. So she turned away toward the chapel. At the very door of the convent, Margaret Fleming intercepted her.

"Didn't I do a good job for you?"

Precisely what job had Margaret done? Whatever it had been, it deserved thanks and she must give it. She mumbled something incoherently, and Margaret went on.

"You got what you wanted, didn't you? And it was just peachy of you to go to bat for me, too."

"Did I? How?"

"Pretend you don't know! Getting my wedding march, of course."

"Are you? I mean, did I? How?"

"What you said."

What in the name of heaven had she said to help Margaret with "Here Comes the Bride?" she asked herself.

"You told me over the phone that as long as it didn't mean anything to me, it didn't matter. Don't you remember?"

"Yes. I remember. I did say that."

"The Monsignor was a doll. He said as long as you didn't care and didn't bring the subject up, I could have it; and I think you're a honey. Anything else I can do about this art stuff, just let me know."

So Sister Gervaise went into the chapel and knelt before the not-so-bad madonna that was there, and she prayed, "Our Lady of the Transition, help us!"

Chapter 14

ONE RUMOR at least had been true. They knew it that June night in the refectory when they saw Mother Bernardine's empty place, heard the reader hurrying through the scripture and martyrology to get to the announcements, and saw Mother Dolorosa nervously picking at the piece of paper that held the news and their fate.

They dared not look up too much because the Provincial, Mother Mary of Mount Carmel, was here in her seat of honor, obviously to begin the visitation. Everything would be thrown into chaos with a new Superior to be installed, for that is what the notice would mean, and on top of that, the visitation of the community. What way was that to run things?

Who would their new Mother be? Obviously, one of their own number, since no stranger was among them. Had there been an outsider coming, she would have been seated at the right of the empty place ready to move in. But there was only Mother Dolorosa, too old now, sitting there as acting Superior. Then who was it?

There was one other absence, but that could be accounted for. Sister Drusilda, who was Assistant Superior, would normally make the announcement but she was not present. Clearly, though, she had gone as companion to Mother

Bernardine—no, Sister Bernardine, now—to whatever place her new assignment would obedience her. Sister Drusilda's absence, however, also meant another thing: it eliminated her as the new Superior since she would have had to be here to accept the chair.

The little sidelong glances swept around. No one ate very much. The soup went cold and was taken away. Who looked nervous? Everybody. It was such a young community. Really there were only two eligibles, Sister Emily and Sister Gervaise. Gervaise was still a little young—and Emily? Oh no, not Emily. Please, God, let it be Gervaise! Please exert your retroactive will and make the Council have decided on Sister Gervaise.

There was still one other. Sister Inez. What in the world would it be like to be under Sister Inez?

But at least, they all thought, there was one blessing. Wouldn't it have been too bad if the transfer had happened last week, and wasn't it providential that Mother Bernardine's call had not come till now? Suppose she had just slipped out while they were all disturbed with her. What an unpleasant ending that would have been—an unhappy memory after nearly five years here. Because she had been a good Superior. Honestly, you couldn't find a better. She had her faults, but who of us hasn't? And her faults were all external. There was nothing the matter with Mother Bernardine. Please, dear Lord, make the new Superior half as kind, half as understanding. Please let her be brave; to be able to say no to bishops; to try to lift the burden of work from us, as Mother Bernardine has done. Please let her be humble enough to acknowledge her faults, big enough to reverse imprudent decisions.

I wish she hadn't gone.

I wish I hadn't made it unpleasant for her.

Bother that old canon law. When you get a good one, why can't you keep her?

I'm so glad it didn't happen a week ago. So glad we had that little talk.

Who will be on my side now? Who will say I should get my vows? She was for me. Despite everything. Despite my unruly tongue. She believed in me. Who now?

Thank God I didn't make an issue of that madonna thing. Thank God I was on her side during that silly business about the dog.

A week ago they had all been angry with the Superior. Even little Sister Consolata's eyes had refused to meet hers and Sister Roseanne looked as if she would like to say something but was learning religious self-control. They were angry with her. Even Sister Inez.

When Mother Bernardine had gone to the infirmary to see her, Sister Inez had said, "Reveraind Muzzer, you should not have done this to me. No."

"But I did it *for* you. I thought it better . . ."

"Now all my Seestairs, they hate me!"

It was somewhat exaggerated, of course, and Mother Bernardine did her best to soothe the distrait nerves. But Sister Inez was Spanish and not to be soothed. She would not say that the Superior was right.

All through the house it had been the same. No one said anything, and they did not hate Sister Inez. No. They were angry with her, Mother Bernardine.

She was glad. She could not explain it but somehow during those next few days she was glad. There was a sense of satisfaction now, and a knowledge that the tension of the last weeks had broken. Positive anger with her was better, she felt, than the suppressed disapproval of the past. Almost, she reveled in it, and even the thought that she might leave them with this feeling about her did not distress her as much as it might have.

Why? Had she really grown into what she had prayed for and had thought hopeless? Once the idea had been only words to her: O Lord, let me share in contumely and all evil judgments about me. Let me bear with you the evil opinion of men. She had thought that she could never really mean those words. But she had, after all, hadn't she? How good that was.

She took no smug satisfaction from the discovery. She said to herself very practically, "Well, it's about time." She said to herself: "If you stay in religion long enough, you're bound to learn something, even if there are times when you don't feel you're getting anywhere." She said very simply, "Thanks, dear Lord."

In the community, too, something was happening. Work which had been done conscientiously was now attacked with fervor. Sometimes, when she was not near, she could hear the old laughter ring out. Of course, that came between waves of controlled and carefully suppressed antagonism, but the antagonism was all focused on herself and the community seemed to have drawn itself together in a coherent unity which it had not had before.

In the presence of the Blessed Sacrament her mind said, "I know that this was the way. I have read often enough that my God is a jealous God. Possibly, though I was unaware of it, I did have my heart set on a poor pet instead of on my beloved Sisters. Now, O Lord, accept this little sacrifice."

182 ✍

That was what her mind said and the words sounded all right as she said them. They were according to all the ascetic books. Free your heart from attachments and you will be free. She had done so, and she was free. But still and all, there was not the same awareness of completeness in this as there was in her acceptance of a new unpopularity. She had not, she thought, progressed beyond abnegation; there was still acceptance and desire. In this, she had not as yet discovered the deeper core of meaning for which all her soul was striving.

It kept her balanced and she was glad. One thing knowingly attained; another still to work on. There was more to discover. "O Lord, that I may see."

Four days had gone by like that. Foolishly, she had been mooning around near Lady's kennel, thinking of nothing, to be sure, certainly not of the dog. But why should she be here?

Then she heard a bark and something not so much like a whine as a song of delight, and a great body bounded upon her and she had Lady in her arms. Sixty miles from Warpath! The pads of the dog's feet must be sore. But here —at St. Rita's!

In a moment she was sitting in a very undignified position on the ground beside the dog. Lady's head was nuzzling into her shoulder. Lady's wet tongue licked her cheek. Then suddenly, while she was still holding her, the dog stopped, shivered, lay down. Lady's head went between her paws, one eye came up, an ashamed eye, with the shame that only a dog can show. Yet her tail wagged ingratiatingly, as if she knew what the ultimate outcome would be.

"So you know," Mother Bernardine said firmly. "At last you know you were a bad dog. You shouldn't eat lilies. You shouldn't knock Spanish ladies down. And you shouldn't have come back from Warpath."

The Superior laughed aloud. The expression now was one of perfect contrition, love and sorrow for sin.

"That's all right," she said. "It is good to be wrong, so awfully good to be wrong."

She looked up when she saw the nuns coming out into the garden, knowing that they would find her there, sitting on the ground, with her arm around Lady's neck.

Sister Emily, of all people, spoke spontaneously, girlishly. "Oh! Reverend Mother! Thanks! You brought Lady back to us."

Mother Bernardine looked at her assembled nuns, her dear daughters in the Lord, and she could not deceive them.

"No," she said, "I didn't. I should have, but I didn't have sense enough to do that. Lady disobeyed me and she came back all on her own."

A man's laughter, unexpected and flurrying, broke in upon them.

"Not quite. I'm sorry to spoil your story. It's a good dog story. But you can't believe all you hear. I had something to do with it."

Oh, goodness, what a fright! But it was nothing. Only Father Fleury from Warpath. "I couldn't keep her. I had a pretty sick dog on my hands. She wouldn't eat, you know."

Sister Roseanne cried: "She only eats lilies! Get her a lily."

Baffled, Father Fleury went away, shaking his head. He did not understand women. Not even Lady.

Then Mother Bernardine said to her Sisters: "I don't know how you could have stood me all these months."

It was Mother Dolorosa who spoke for them. "There was

184 ✍

nothing the matter with you, Mother. It was all our fault, I guess. You never did anything wrong."

"That's what I mean." Her hand played with the consoled head of Lady. How could they all have stood it? "I never did anything wrong. I kept asking, didn't I, and you kept telling me? I examined my conscience and I couldn't find anything wrong. That—why, that's unendurable. You might have faults, but I didn't. Not one. Not a teeny, weeny, single, little fault."

She stood up then, her eyes shining, with Lady at her side. It was solved! Nor would she be doing this for herself. Why hadn't she thought of that? She would be going. Was there any reason in the world why she couldn't give them Lady?

"And now," she added at last, "I am going to do something very wrong. Tell Sister Inez. Something utterly, absolutely imprudent and worse."

They all knew, of course, before she told them, and their laughter was due to the Cause of Our Joy.

"You are going to keep Lady."

They should have known from that *you*. It was a dead giveaway but somehow it had escaped them, and they had not really known until they saw the empty place—until the announcement came.

The martyrology was over at last. The reader slipped into her place and Mother Dolorosa took the lectern.

"According to a decision of the Council of Venerables of the Sisters of the Amiable Heart of Mary and in accord with the Canon Law of the Holy and Apostolic Catholic Church, let it be officially declared that with the ratification by and approval of the Archbishop of Sheraton, Very Reverend

Mother Mary of Mount Carmel Mahan is hereby released from her office as Provincial . . ."

No longer the Provincial? Then what? Who? Who?

". . . and is to be replaced in office by Mother Bernardine of St. Francis Hartigan, to whom, as from this date, all of Ours shall owe obedience as to their Provincial Superior."

Mother Bernardine, Provincial? No one had guessed that. But no one!

They had all made a noise with their breaths, then were suddenly silent.

The notice continued. "By order of Very Reverend Mother Provincial Bernardine of St. Francis, Mother Agnes Marie Gow of Marycliff College, Sheraton, is hereby relieved of her office as Superior and President of that house and college and shall repair to the motherhouse as Reverend Mistress of Novices. By further appointment of Very Reverend Mother Provincial, the office of President of the College and Superior of the House at Marycliff, Sheraton, shall from this date forward be occupied by Mother Mary Drusilda Ritchie."

Drusilda! The last one anyone would have thought of. She'd never even been a college nun. But a good choice when one thought of it. Drusilda was a financial wizard. That's what was needed now at the Cliffs.

All very exciting. But what about St. Rita's? For them?

The "by orders of" and "ratified by" went on. Then it came. Mother Mount Carmel moved over into the vacant seat of the Superior. She smiled at them. She said, *"Deo Gratias,"* which meant that they might talk.

Mother Mount Carmel! Sister Gervaise's heart leaped. She looked across the refectory to catch the eye of one who would be as delighted as she, and yes, Sister Roseanne was smiling at her. There was such relief in Roseanne's eyes. She would be safe now. She would get her vows. This woman, this great woman, understood her even better, yes, even better than had Mother Bernardine. No one would ask her to leave because she couldn't be a dray horse. She didn't want to leave. She wanted to stay and conquer her faults and reach perfection. All the terrors that had haunted Sister Roseanne seemed to evaporate. She didn't have a headache now. It was just as if a weight had been lifted.

For herself, Sister Gervaise experienced almost the same joy. Mother Mount Carmel had been her Mistress of Novices years before. She had been her constant model, almost idol, in the years between. She had been her beloved Provincial for the last six years. And now she was coming here as her own Mother! How good could God be?

Oh, she knew what criticisms or, rather, doubts, there might be from the others who did not know. They would say that Mother had never been a high-school nun. What would she know about running affairs on this level without any experience? College nuns had a totally different life: more glamorous, perhaps, more privileged, sometimes more proud. Would college nuns know how to deal with pastors, having been spared all that? Could they come down to the level of teenage problems without seeming to condescend? Would they realize that because of the work and routine and long class hours, high-school nuns needed a little more leniency in the house itself?

Of course Mother Mount Carmel would realize it. Sister Gervaise answered the objections before they were raised. She was a very wonderful woman. She could manage anything. Mother Bernardine had been marvelous, but now— what a year they would have!

What a year they would have?

They would talk about the Washington Merry-Go-Round, the rotation in office. Wasn't there any new blood? Did the same group have to stay in administrative positions all the time, merely changing places with one another? If you had someone ideal you wouldn't want to waste her, would you? Why didn't they do what the Jesuits do: put the Superiors back in the classroom for a while, so they'd get the feeling of the crowd again?

They weren't Jesuits, that's why. And why should all nuns think they were Jesuits? The Society of Jesus didn't have any women in it and there was no sense in trying to live like a man. The Jesuits were all right, but they weren't women.

And by the way, there *was* new blood. Sister Drusilda—no, Mother Drusilda now—she was new blood. You never even had thought of her. And she was a high-school nun who was becoming a college president. Wasn't that enough for you?

Wouldn't you rather have Mother Mount Carmel—what an honor for little St. Rita's—than Mother Drusilda?

No. She just mustn't think of that. It could not be that one little part even, of her rejoicing, was that her Superior was not to be the former bursar, or that the bursar had been moved, or that she wouldn't have to live under or even with that excellent person, that fine businesswoman, Mother Drusilda. Her rejoicing must be all positive, sheer happiness that Mother Mount Carmel would be theirs.

Mother Drusilda was a good religious. She would be an excellent executive, a superb disciplinarian, a fine example in her community. She would build and pay for what she had built. She would do a lot of good for the community and for the college itself at the Cliffs. She would be just dandy—at the Cliffs.

Sister Gervaise was glad, nonetheless, that it would be the Cliffs that would benefit, and that Mother Drusilda was not to be the Superior at St. Rita's. She had to be honest. She had to admit it.

She looked over and smiled at Mother Mount Carmel but the Superior had turned away, talking to Mother Dolorosa, and did not see her.

Oh well. There would be a whole year to tell her how happy she was that she was here with them.

Chapter 15

EVERYTHING must be done right if for no other reason than to please Reverend Mother. The spiritual books said that that was not a good motive and, in general, they were right, but this was different. It was a good enough motive for now.

Sister Gervaise took inventory and only one remissness stood out. She had had those full-length mirrors installed in Sister Emily's classroom, and she had been after Mr. MacGill to remove them for nearly three weeks now. They were still there. It wasn't her fault, actually, but she certainly was responsible for them.

It was always a problem to find Mr. MacGill but today it seemed harder than ever. She knew that when all else failed there was always the boiler room, but that was sacrosanct, and weird rumors had come to her about the reception any-one received who dared track Mr. MacGill to his lair.

It just had to be done. The unfamiliar pipes above her head in Mr. MacGill's basement seemed to menace her. The white-clad furnaces were not friendly like the ones she was accustomed to. But she found the boiler room and from the reek of pipe tobacco gathered that Mr. MacGill was indeed within.

He did not answer her first knock. She knew he was there. She rapped harder.

To her third knock she heard an irate, "Yeah?"

"I want to see you."

"O.K. Hold your horses."

She did not know what he was doing that could possibly take all this time, but as she held her horses she had phantasms of strange and secretive actions within the holy of holies that reminded her of the old days when, as a girl, she would stand outside her father's dressing room while he hid things. Tidied things up, he would say. At last Mr. MacGill mumbled something.

"What did you say?"

"I ast who was there."

"It's me." What a stupid thing to say! She wasn't a little girl trying to reach her father. "Sister Gervaise."

"Whadda you want?"

"I want to see you."

"Come around later."

"No."

"Whadda you say?"

"Open up that door!" Come now, control yourself. This is no way to act when you want a favor done. Favor? This was no favor. She wanted a janitor to do his job.

At last he opened the door. She had a speedy glimpse of a red-tiled floor, a heap of newspapers looking as if they were concealing another heap of things possibly made out of glass, and an incredibly spindly rocker beside them. Then the door closed with them both outside.

"Well?"

She drew in her breath hard and pulled her shoulders back. It always helped her self-control. Her voice, she was delighted to discover, was low and nunlike.

❧ 191

"I wonder if you could help me? You know, we have to get those mirrors down from Sister Emily's classroom."

"Why now?"

"Because there are exams coming." She just thought of that in time! "So perhaps if I could help you . . ."

"Not a chance today, Sister. Gotta get the windows washed!"

"What did you say?" Why wasn't he washing them then?

"I said, not a chance. I got work to do."

"So I see!" Oh, please be careful! "Look, Mr. MacGill. I asked you quite some time ago to take those mirrors down . . ."

"What did you put 'em up for?"

"So you march right upstairs and take them down. Right now."

"Who do you think you're talking to?"

"You. And it's none of your business why I put them up. Now get!" She shouldn't. Who did she think he was, one of her students? But he got. He actually went upstairs and, as she discovered later, finally took down the mirrors.

It was a few days later, when she heard him talking to Father Rolfe, that she realized what she had done, particularly after Father Rolfe laughed. She was to remember that later.

What a Hitler I am, she thought. I'm becoming a real schoolteacher, treating everyone as if he were in seventh grade. I've seen that happen to others. Never dreamed it would to myself. Mustn't. Mustn't.

She could not allow the day to pass without making amends. But how did you go about making amends to Mr. MacGill? The thought of a spiritual bouquet tastefully decorated with small sheep and wheat sheaves crossed her mind and she laughed out loud at the very idea. You could not associate Mr. MacGill with such things. If I could only slip him a jug, she thought irreverently. And yet—Mr. MacGill needed prayers and he was going to get them whether he wanted them or not.

She had on her desk a spiritual bouquet card that Sister Consolata had decorated for her; one to be used in an emergency. It was particularly frilly and looked very much like a valentine. There was even a puff-ball lamb on it. But it had room for Masses, prayers and aspirations, and all you had to do was to fill it in.

Sister Gervaise filled it in and, once more making the journey down to the basement, slipped the puff-ball lamb under Mr. MacGill's boiler-room door.

Afterward, when she thought about it, it made her feel a little silly and, because Mr. MacGill never referred to it, she became, for a while, somewhat self-conscious in his presence. What she did not know was that the custodian pasted the bouquet on the wall of his sanctum to which no profane eye would ever penetrate, and, having seen it there, removed some of the more atrocious pinups that had previously adorned the walls. That lamb hung there, getting somewhat yellower, until the day of his death. It was the only spiritual bouquet that Mr. MacGill had ever received.

All the hours now were taken up with the final preparations for examinations and for the graduation exercises. There was one other thing to look forward to but that did not bother her very much. Superiors might be changed at any time, but it was the custom in the Midwestern province to make all changes in the assignments of non-superiors on the same day, usually just before the high-school commencements, so that the nuns would be able to tell their charges whether or not they would be with them next year. In their own household slang the Sisters called these changes "salads," the derivation of which word was lost, although it had probably come from the first word of the older French briefs.

But since Sister Gervaise had had a long chat with Mother Mount Carmel about plans for the coming year, she had no fears for herself from the "salads." The only way the changes in status could affect her personally was through the shifts that might be made in the personnel of the community. A replacement was needed for Sister Drusilda; Sister Roseanne would return to the novitiate for her vows and then would probably come back here; Sister Emily was in constant readiness to do God's will wherever obedience or necessity dictated, but was as much of a fixture here, in all actuality, as she was herself; and Sister Consolata had a worried look, as if she had had some hint of an impending uprooting.

For the rest, they were pretty certain to remain, and lately the policy seemed to be to keep the Sisters in one place as long as possible. It was better that way than moving them all about all the time. How could you expect to have a good alumni if there were no one at the old school to return to?

Now that Mother Mount Carmel had approved her dramatic plans for next season, all she needed was ratification by the Monsignor. Might as well get that done and over with. Then she could spend the summer planning and making her script books. Nobody knew how many hours of work went into that, hours that could be wasted during rehearsal time unless you had everything figured out and planned beforehand. Of course, since you did this at your desk in your room, it did not count. Only the things people saw you do counted as work.

One day after lunch—there were to be no exams that

afternoon—she slipped over to the rectory. It seemed to be a good time to catch the Monsignor at home; he always was sprawled out in his easy chair listening to the radio.

He looked up when she came in. "So it's yourself," he said by way of greeting. "I was going to send for you one of these days."

"Here I am." She smiled. "I've got the plans for the shows for next year with me."

He glanced casually at her list. "Where's my St. Patrick's night?" he asked.

That was the trouble. If you did a thing once it immediately became a custom.

"I thought that was special."

"It sure is. You know it's a funny thing about St. Patrick. He has a feast day every year. It's always special."

"Well, of course, Monsignor, but . . ."

"So I'll just write that in. The black and red ledger in the parish safe." He had boomed out that last sentence so loudly that it made her jump. For a moment she tried to connect it with St. Patrick but she failed. Then she realized he had been addressing Father Rolfe who was in the other room. She could detect fumbling sounds now, as if someone were searching for records. The Monsignor, in his ordinary voice, was going on ". . . the best thing you ever did."

Would she never get away from that? It would hurt her always.

"Oh, I don't mind," she said. "Of course I'll do it." She had just committed a host of nuns for generations to come till the end of time to taking on an extra assignment. The realization struck her with full force. You just don't commit yourself; you commit all your successors. It wasn't fair.

"Sure, you'll do it. But wouldn't it be nice just once in a

while if your old pastor didn't have to get down on his knees to you?"

She did not feel that the probability was great. "I'll be glad to do it. Can I have that little boy Stanley again?"

Monsignor Cooney shook his head in negation. "The grade school's letting him take his exams at home this year, if you see what I mean."

She understood.

She was the first to break the silence. "You wanted to see me about something else, Monsignor?"

The pastor roused himself. "Mmm. You know that Fleming wedding next week?"

She did, indeed.

"Well, against my better judgment I gave in to you about that Lohengrin thing. But I don't like it."

"You don't?" This was a reversal, indeed.

"I don't mean the tune. It's the principle of the thing. The Bishop doesn't like to be crossed. But it isn't that so much either. It's that you can't do one thing for one parishioner and another for another. There's a lot of pressure on me, and I just want you to know what you got me into."

"Me? I got you into? What in the world did I have to do with it?" She was on her feet now.

"Plenty. So all I have to say to you, Sister, is be careful. You'll only mess things up if you interfere. That goes for everything. I know you mean well but—now take that Morrison case. Better not poke your nose into that any more. It's no business for a nun at all."

What was a nun's business? Just to teach school? Not to give advice when it was asked? And here she had been resolving to do more of that next year, accusing herself of giving too little time to counseling.

196 ☞

"Very well, Monsignor." She turned away. Better to say nothing. Better just to take it and offer it up. Although there was plenty to say. . . .

He dismissed her then and she did her best, too, to stay out of all the affairs of the parish. It was not her fault if she couldn't quite manage it.

She had been silent that night at recreation when the subject turned, as it tended to at this time of year, to religious vocations among the girls. Somebody asked her if Theresa Doyle wasn't thinking of entering the convent, and she just said that she didn't think so, not even adding that Theresa was thinking far more of Joe Maguire.

Then came Sister Emily's bombshell.

"I think you should all know," she said, her face outlined in stained glass, "that a lovely little girl of ours is entering the novitiate this summer."

She had the attention of all now.

"It came as a surprise to me, although I have suspected it for some time. Now, since it's all settled, I feel free to tell you."

Her freedom did not force her into any immediacy of revelation. Sister Emily held her moment. Finally she said, "It's dear little Rosemary Morrison."

There was a flutter and exclamations and reasonable joy. Only Sister Gervaise stood up. She said "No!"

They all turned to look at her.

Sister Emily was most distressed. "What did you say, Sister?"

"I know her pretty well. She mustn't."

"Mustn't? Why?"

"Because she hasn't any vocation."

Sister Emily's smile was tolerant now and her eyes were not reproving, but she said, "That is for God to decide."

Sister Gervaise said no more. It was hard work to control herself but she did. They would all think that she disapproved of Rosemary because she ran around with boys, because she liked pretty things and a little lipstick now and then. That wasn't the reason at all. It was precisely because Jeanne Collins didn't do these things that she doubted about her vocation. As for Rosemary—well—let them think what they wanted to. She had her own ideas. She wouldn't interfere.

Furthermore, she had no intention of seeing Mrs. Morrison. She couldn't very well be rude, though, could she, when two days later her call bell rang and they told her that Mrs. Morrison was waiting for her in the parlor? Seculars could say they were not at home; what could a nun say in the evening? She was at home all right. Where else would she be? She more or less had to go down. But she would say nothing. She would keep out of this this time.

Mrs. Morrison did not smile when the nun entered but there was something different about her attitude. She was, as usual, nothing if not direct.

"I told you before, Sister, that I wasn't going to bring this subject up again. I've changed my mind. I thought you were absolutely on the other side."

"I'm on no side," Sister Gervaise said.

"I heard differently. I am informed that you are opposed to Rosemary's entering the convent."

"I am."

"Why?"

"Because I don't think she has a vocation. I'll be as frank as you are. I think it would be just an escape, like the time she wanted to go away to boarding school in the middle of the term."

"You encouraged her in that."

"No. Not exactly. I just didn't put any obstacles in her way."

"Why?"

"I wanted her to change her own mind. If you make a thing difficult for youngsters, they just want that thing more."

Mrs. Morrison shook her head. "I see. In fact, I agree with you. And whether you know it or not, you're on my side."

Sister Gervaise did try to stop the other woman from giving her any confidences, but Mrs. Morrison had made up her mind and there was no halting her now. "I'm sorry," she said. "Things have gone so far that you have a duty to know. You've heard my husband. You've listened to Rosemary. Now we'd better get down to some facts."

The facts, as presented by Mrs. Morrison, were not so highly colored as Sister Gervaise had expected. It was a pretty straightforward story as it was told. It was the struggle of a woman, through the years, to adjust herself to a basically materialistic husband—oh, a good man, no doubt, a good provider, a solid family man. If he spoiled Rosemary and left all the discipline to his wife, that, too, was a mere excess of devotion—and came about because the wife was the more dominant character.

But she couldn't discuss anything with him. She had given that up long ago. For years she had merely stated her conclusions; it did not make for domestic felicity but it was better than the wrangling and blustering which once had disturbed their home. Then Rosemary had begun to grow up.

Mr. Morrison had been right. Things had got worse instead of better.

The Nick Collasanto case, for instance. Snobbery? Well, maybe. But among Mrs. Morrison's ambitions for her daughter was that she should be a lady. "The language that she picked up. The attitudes! My husband never even noticed those things. I don't say that Nick isn't a fine boy, but I didn't want Rosemary to be in the rock-and-roll set. Was that wrong of me? And I didn't force Joe Maguire on her. She liked Joe. And his parents see eye to eye on what teen-agers do. I think Joe's healthy for her. Is that being a snob?"

Then suddenly, in the midst of her romances, Rosemary had announced that she wanted to be a nun.

"Do you see the position that put me in? I am the one that reads spiritual books, who makes a meditation every day. But I know my daughter. She doesn't want to go to the convent. She just wants to get away from home. Anything would do. And she knows how I feel. I would automatically be the one to stand out against her. I had to listen to Sister Emily every day. It made me the worldly mother and Rose-mary—why, Rosemary is really more like her father than she is like me." It was as close as Mrs. Morrison came to saying that Rosemary was worldly also, and Sister Gervaise re-spected her for her reticence. "Anything she wanted, par-ticularly if I was opposed to it, her father would go along with. Sometimes I thought—maybe it was wrong of me—that the whole thing was done just to aggravate me. So there we were. He was on the side of religion now; I was against my girl's vocation. Then I thought maybe it was the influence of the nuns, your influence, Sister."

"Mine?"

"I even spoke to the Monsignor about it. I thought if I

could get her away to some college where there were no nuns—but I was afraid of the danger. I wanted to be nearby. I thought, too, if she did not have her father near her . . . Sister, this is going to sound sentimental."

"There's no harm in that."

Mrs. Morrison's tone was far from sentimental. She sounded like Sister Drusilda. "I thought I might win back my daughter."

"But it isn't right to leave your husband like that."

"I know. At least I know it now. He told you what he accused me of. I wish it weren't true. But he was right. I hadn't thought of it that way. I faced it out. It was an escape for me. I know, too, how it must have sounded to you. 'A woman of the Pharisees,'" she said. "I hate Mauriac.

"And so," she concluded after a pause, "you probably still disapprove of me. Sister Emily does."

"She implied that you agreed to Rosemary's entering the convent."

"Agreed? Yes. I suppose so. I always agree when I am defeated. I learned to do that long ago. I know all the other things about myself: that my church work is a substitution reaction, sublimation, maybe; that my self-control is just expediency. I know all the words. I know, finally, that I was trying to run away from my problems. And so is Rosemary. But if she runs away to a convent she can always get out of it. If she runs away with a boy . . . She might, you know."

"Yes. She might. And this is better."

"Not good, but better."

That might be the motto of your life, Sister Gervaise thought, as Mrs. Morrison left. And of mine. And of so many in our time. It was not enough. Then, too, she reflected, it about summed up her own reactions to Mrs. Morrison. She still did not like her very much, but better. She did not approve of all her attitudes, she did not understand them fully, but better.

Her own community, she thought as she looked around at them later, were not saints. They were just better than most seculars, she supposed. Merely better. That was no boast. It was their duty to be better. But where were the saints?

"Better. Not great love, but some. Enough. Pretty good."

The thought had come back to Sister Gervaise as she heard the wedding march drifting across from the church. Margaret and Jim. Not great love. But enough. Pretty good. Had she given the right advice?

She supposed so, although she would be chary of giving any advice in the future. The Monsignor had met her only once, had shaken his head at her and said, "I hear you talked to Mrs. Morrison," and still shaking his head in hurt wonderment, had walked away.

Yet what else would she have said? To Mrs. Morrison? To Margaret? Take life as it comes. Accept the facts. Make the best of things.

No!

With a sudden flash it came to her. This was the advice she had been giving to others for so long now. How had she got into the habit of those words? She did not live by them herself. Do not accept! Hold out for the best! Never give up! Count each defeat only as a battle toward a victory at the end! That's how she lived. She knew it. And in the future she would say it, honestly, come what might! Live valiantly!

"The Kingdom of Heaven suffereth violence and the violent bear it away."

Once that had been her motto. It would be again. Nor would she confuse modesty and humility with cowardice, nor prudence with craven fear. She would defy everything and shake some sense into Rosemary.

Soon she would know how it was turning out with Margaret. It was the custom of the most loyal of the alumnae to come right over to the convent after Mass to pay a visit to the chapel and to hold a little reception for the nuns so that they might see the bride in her wedding dress. A nice custom, and Margaret would not fail them.

Just as she thought the Mass must be almost over, Sister Consolata, breathless, tracked her down. "Know what I heard?"

She did not know.

"The 'salads' are in the house. Reverend Mother's going to put up the list this morning!"

It was true, too, and it almost spoiled Margaret's reception, for the nuns kept filing out to take a peek at the list, and some did not return. Sister Gervaise, trampling down her curiosity, loyally stayed with the bridal couple.

She even got a chance to speak to Margaret alone, not for long, but long enough.

"How is it?" she asked. "How do you feel?"

All brides look beautiful, but Margaret was stunning. Particularly now.

"Wonderful," she whispered back.

"Good. I'm glad."

"I fell in love."

"Did you? That's fine. When?"

"Last night. It all went just the opposite from the books. I just all of a sudden fell in love. When I tried on my dress. It made it all come real. Crazy?"

"Perhaps. But wonderful."

"Oh yes! And you told me it didn't matter romantically."

"Maybe I was wrong. Maybe it does matter."

"I think so."

She kissed Sister Gervaise, took a lily out of her bouquet and gave it to the nun. Then she was off.

Out of the acceptance of the lesser things had come the great thing. Confusing. Maybe there lay a halfway truth between the extremes. Maybe one could find it someday.

Absent-mindedly, still holding the lily, Sister Gervaise made her way to the *tabella* where the status was hung, sheet upon sheet of it. All the other nuns had seen it and had departed to buzz about its implications, its effect upon themselves.

Almost without interest, Sister Gervaise found her own convent heading. St. Rita's. *Mittendi.*

Suddenly and literally she was almost bowled over. That dog! Lady had jumped for the lily. Go away. Go away now! But she had scarcely felt anything at all, inside or out. On the status, under changes, was her own name.

Leaving: Sister Gervaise Rhodes, to Professor of Poetry and Drama at Marycliff College.

Chapter 16

Sᴉꜱᴛᴇʀ ɢᴇʀᴠᴀɪꜱᴇ read the congratulatory telegram from her father again. It was ironic and she scarcely knew how to answer it, pointing, as it did, to the wide gulf that separated them now. She had been so close to him once. But the distance between them was not merely physical; they lived in different worlds.

He was on one of his tours, constantly and professionally young, always the leading man, never the star. Proud of her in a way. "My little daughter in the convent," he had said. It made her seem like a child in pigtails and boarding-school uniform. And now, because of the change, he would revise his formula. "My daughter at the College of Our Lady of the Cliffs (he never got Marycliff right) . . . one of the best drama departments in the West." The West began with Jersey.

Why, he might even accept character parts in the future.

She knew the typed message by heart. He was proud of her having made good. She and her talents had been recognized at last. She was going to teach in college next fall.

Her heart kept crying out to him: "I don't want to be changed. It isn't an honor. We don't have honors. It's just another assignment." And her mind, or a mean little corner of it, kept whispering the old politician's phrase, "kicked upstairs."

They did not want her here any more. St. Rita's didn't want her any more.

In the three days since the assignment had come, even during the graduation that she had physically attended, she had been fighting down the imaginings of an Oppenheim intrigue that was forcing her out. Nobody had been able to help her much in her struggles for spiritual thinking and pure motivation.

Mrs. Doyle, Theresa's mother, had come around to the convent and voiced the sentiments of the town. "We can't lose you," she had said. "Theresa is heartbroken. And Charlie. Just as he was getting ready to have you in high school!"

"I know. I'll be sorry to miss him."

"We're thinking of making up a petition. Should we send it to the Bishop or who?"

"To nobody. It wouldn't help. I have to go where I'm sent, you know."

"But we don't have to let you." The brown eyes snapped with outraged loyalty. "You've got your rules and you have to live by them. But they aren't our rules." Then she paused and a hurt expression came over her face. "Don't you want to stay?"

What answer was there? All her heart wanted to say how deeply she desired to stay. This had become her town. These were her people, her children. She knew them all. Whom would they go to now? What of the romances she had patched up? The marriages she had kept together? The scandals she had averted? Even the converts she had made?

Oh yes. She had deep spiritual reasons for wanting to stay. Aloud she said, and truthfully, "I've got to be obedient."

"Don't you like us here?"

"Yes. Yes. You're making it hard for me. I want what God wants." It sounded stuffy and nunlike. But then, she didn't suppose there was anything wrong with a nun sounding like a nun.

"What God wants?" Mrs. Doyle sniffed. "You mean what that new Provincial of yours wants. Believe me, I knew that one when she was here. She just wants to drag you away with her so as to build up the Cliffs. What's Mother Mount Carmel thinking of to let you go? That Mother Bernardine, she's an ambitious woman. She's just grabbing you away from us now she's Provincial. She's had her eye on you right along."

For a moment Sister Gervaise smiled. Mother Bernardine had had her eye on her all right. Last thing she had done was to call her into her office to tell her to get her dramatic gear out of Emily's cupboard. That was just before she was made Provincial, right after all that nonsense about the dog.

"She just probably needs somebody at the Cliffs," Sister Gervaise said.

"Nonsense. No, she takes *you* away from us right after she takes Sister Drusilda. She was a good businesswoman. We need a good businesswoman here at Wolf's Head just as much as they do at Sheraton."

You know a lot about the convent, Sister Gervaise thought. As much as Mrs. Morrison does. I wonder how much of your knowledge is my fault? Have I revealed too much of our interior discipline? Is that the reason why Mother Mount Carmel isn't keeping me? Aloud she said, "Mother

Drusilda will be a good Superior at the Cliffs. She's a builder."

It was reparation for what she had thought, for she remembered with remorse the relief she had felt when she had learned that Sister Drusilda was leaving them to be Reverend Mother at the Cliffs. Not that there was anything the matter with Mother Drusilda, really. Just that they had never seen eye to eye, the bursar and the dramatic nun. They had had different viewpoints on matters of money, disbursements for dramatics, questions of art, things like that. Personality difficulties. She herself had really been glad when she heard that the bursar was departing. Really glad. It was wrong of her. Well, there was one thing she could be sure of, and that was that Mother Drusilda had not asked for her to join her community.

Apparently Mrs. Doyle felt that she was getting nowhere. She rose to go.

"They're just ruining St. Rita's," she said. "And I tell you it will kill my Theresa."

It probably would, Sister Gervaise reflected as she said good-by. Theresa had been her shadow for so many years. But there was a special reason now. Theresa was sixteen this year, entering the senior class, and had already been appointed lead in the class play. Wasn't that reason enough? With a new moderator in, who could tell? Everything would be changed, even poor Theresa's play. Everything they had built would collapse. Father Cooney—Monsignor—might make them have minstrel shows again.

Monsignor. The priests. Was that it? She remembered what had been said about interfering. There had been that business about insisting on good Catholic theatre. Then her flop: *Murder in the Cathedral*. Opposing the parish entertainments that made all the money; the Lohengrin episode; her support of Mr. Alemando's modernistic statue. Hadn't she been warned then? Mother Bernardine had told her not to tread so often on Monsignor Cooney's toes. But Mother Bernardine was stuck with her then, and the first thing she had done when she got the authority was to take her away from St. Rita's and the Monsignor's toes.

Then there was the time when she had to get those mirrors out of 3-B and she had ordered Mr. MacGill to help her. It was dangerous to give commands to a custodian. You begged, entreated, sometimes bribed, but you did not order him about. She had heard him say to Father Rolfe that day, "That one thinks she's the pastor." And Father Rolfe had laughed. Sympathetically.

Yes. It was the clergy and Mr. MacGill. Between them they had railroaded her. Or maybe it was Mrs. Morrison, after all.

Oh dear. Here she was, doing it again. Attributing motives. Her father's telegram had got her mixed up again and mooning around instead of going down to chapel to prepare for confession. The Extraordinary Visitor was due today, too. He was Father Fleury from Warpath. She would put Mrs. Doyle and her petition out of her mind and lay her full oblation before the Lord.

In her preparation for confession she determined to be explicit about her suspicions, her lack of interior acceptance of the commands of superiors, and of allowing herself to dwell upon worldly reasons for resisting God's will. She was quite clear, if a little long-winded when she confessed, and for her penance Father Fleury gave her one *Hail Mary* and the instruction that she was to reread her Rule on the virtue of Obedience.

She knew it by heart but she read it again anyway.

"A Sister should not murmur in her heart about the commands of Superiors, but as far as the will can bend the understanding, she should try to conform docilely, even in her mind, to the Obediences imposed upon her; nor should she curiously inquire into the motives of those whom God has placed over her, but listen sweetly and humbly, as if to the voice of God. Thus she should go gladly to the appointed place of her assignment, accepting, not with resignation but with joy, those occupations which are enjoined."

Reading the Rule did not help her. She was startled, disturbed at the fact. "As far as the will can bend the understanding." How far could it? No one asked you to thwart the intellect. Your intellect might not be a very good one but it was all you had. It was against human nature not to see reasons for human actions. How far must you go? And the pastor and Mr. MacGill, the custodian, were they her superiors? She could listen sweetly and humbly to the voice of Mother Mount Carmel and hear in it the accents of God. But it was difficult to accept Mr. MacGill's rasp as anything particularly divine.

As a penance imposed on herself she went over to the stage in the gymnasium and began to sort things and tabulate them as well as she could. For her successor. Whoever it might be. She had only five days to clean up this Augean stable. If only she were more like Sister Emily!

Everything here was valuable. To her. To nobody else. To much of this the only reaction would be "rubbish." Here was the old top of a gaslight fixture that she had long envisioned as a crown. Could be made into one. The faded portiere. Last year a door hanging; next year a regal gown. No next year.

She must get at the lists of patrons and weed out the deadheads. Most of them were personal friends of hers. Hard time building up an audience. The technique of interminable telephone calls. Would anybody carry through? Mustn't moon about. Put on the bed-ticking-striped apron and bib and get to work. Couldn't protect the linens at throat and head. Never had been able to. Clean up and sort out the books and screws and braces. Or why bother? Hopeless mess. Throw them out. No. Next year . . . expense . . . poverty . . . obedience.

She worked until her senses swam in the black heat of backstage. This numbness was better. Couldn't remember how dear this town had become to her; how, long after they had happened, even the bitter moments when she had been training early audiences and they had laughed at the wrong things—the mistakes, the teetering scenery—now had become funny and even a little endearing. Because, although they had laughed, they had come back again. To her shows. To her theatre.

She straightened up hurriedly with a catch in her back and a worse catch in her thinking. Hers? Yes. Bother the spiritual grooves of thought. They were hers. Nobody else's. She had made them, trained them, they were hers. This was her town. She didn't care what the books said; you had to face it. Hers. "These are mine." So there! They'll never belong to anybody else. Never. They say the work will go on. It won't. Nobody else will throw herself into it the way I did. Nobody would be that much of a fool.

So was that why God was pulling her out of this? She had been attached. Wasn't that the word the spiritual writers used? In her fatigue, now, it was just a word. I was attached to these things. So what? So I was attached. Wasn't a woman supposed to be attached? Places, people, things, meant something to a real woman. She was supposed to be the center of a little world. Men were the roamers, the hunters, the navigators. Women were intended to cling. Even the Rule. The Holy Rule had been intended first for men. It had just changed he to she. All right for men, but did God want you to change your nature, not to be a woman? Why shouldn't Mrs. Doyle and Theresa and the rest of them want to cling to her? The petition idea was just a bit silly, not because it was not understandable, but because it wouldn't work. It was a woman's way of reacting.

Mechanically she kept busy. She sneezed as the dust from the old stage cloth that she was sweeping rose up like smoke about her.

No. She had never wanted this job. She had not asked for it. She had pleaded time after time that she would prefer not to be in show business. But it was different, being removed at your own request and being pulled out by the roots like this. What was the real reason? "Must not curiously inquire into motives . . ." Why not? Didn't she have a right to know, just for the sake of self-improvement?

Hastily and without reluctance she threw out the gas fixture that would have turned into a crown. It made a loud noise in the tin barrel.

Then, automatically, as she had so many times before, she replied to a voice calling her from the dimness.

"Sister Gervaise!"

"Here I am."

"Where are you?"

"On the stage. Don't trip over the wire coil by the switchboard. You'll see me if you push the traveler aside."

"What's a traveler?"

212 ✍

"That drape you just got through. Oh, it's you. I thought you were one of the girls."

It was little Sister Consolata. When at last Sister Gervaise could get a good look at her, she thought she could detect tears.

"What are you doing? All by yourself! Do you have to do that, too?"

"Yes."

"Oh dear!" Sister Consolata started to sit on the dusty divan, thought better of it, and leaned dangerously against a slantwise stack of scenery. "What'll I ever do?"

"What you've got to do, I suppose, like the rest of us." She did not want to sound sharp, and she added quickly, "Nothing's so bad when you get used to it."

"I'm it."

"You're what?"

"I'm you. I'm the drama department. The house assignments just came out. I've got this, on top of everything. I can't do it, Sister!"

"Of course you can," she said. Speedily, she unrolled some unused canvas and spread it out on the dusty couch. "Sit down here."

"I've got the whole ninth grade, except religion, and afternoon art classes and four hours a week at Marquette, studying, and all the holy cards to paint and the junior choir. And now this! There aren't that many hours."

"No, there aren't. We all have to face that. Every nun in these United States."

"But you know all about this work. Your father and all. And I don't know even the name of those hanging things. Just because I know something about art, they think . . ."

≈ 213

"Just because you can read English, you can write. Just because you aren't a deaf-mute, you can sing. Just because my father is an actor, I'm a director. I know."

"But you were trained."

"That came later. Not at first. I proved how incapable I was so they sent me to Catholic School of the Theatre. I started just as you are starting. Most of us do."

"I haven't even time to say my prayers. Even now."

That was the real trouble, and she had no answer for that. She changed the subject rapidly.

"Look. I have five days. We can skip the cleanup. Get Mr. MacGill to do it. I mean, ask Mr. MacGill to do it. And I'll work with you. We'll go over everything. Then, if you decide what play you're going to do," poor Theresa and her *Mrs. MacThing,* "I can make you a prompt book. That's a copy with directions in it, you know. Any idea what you'd like to put on?"

"Oh, I thought some nice play with a good deal of music in it would be nice."

"Hmmph. At least it isn't a minstrel." Theresa can't sing, she remembered.

"What did you say?"

"Nothing. Never mind. We'll pull you through. I'd offer to come down and help toward dress-rehearsal time but that would never do. Once I'm at the Cliffs, I'd better stay out of here."

"Oh, Sister, how I envy you!" There was no need to add more. It was the myth at St. Rita's, as at any primary or secondary school, that the college Sisters were a breed apart who floated about in an intellectual leisure, teaching classes only twelve hours a week, constantly attending fabulous and distant conventions, meeting all kinds of celebrities, while

214 ✍

the Sisters in the regular schools groaned and droned and disciplined. That it wasn't quite true, Sister Gervaise knew.

"I'll trade with you," she said, laughing for the first time. "Now come on. Get those smudges off your face and I'll show you the prop closet."

Teaching Sister Consolata helped pass the time during the next few days, and all the townspeople were so kind to Sister Gervaise. They sent her gifts until there were enough handkerchiefs, black gloves and shawls to outfit all of St. Rita's for a year. People came over to see her and called her up, until at last she had to tell the portress, "Don't put any calls through to me. Not even if the Pope telephones. I'm busy."

Even Monsignor Cooney had been gruffly pleasant. "Now I'm going," she thought. "Now that he's got me safely out of here, he can afford to be nice." At least, she had the consolation of knowing that it wasn't any of her own Sisters at the convent who had been responsible for her going. "No one wants my job, that's for sure. Least of all the one who got it."

Actually, turning everything over to Sister Consolata was a revelation to herself of how much she had learned. It was amazing the questions she was able to answer about things she had taken for granted for so long. She discovered that, almost automatically, she knew all about how to pro- cure ads for the program, where to steal or borrow furniture, exactly how to approach the women's clubs for mention of the play at their monthly meetings, which electricians would give you the best rentals on transformers, how much coolade should be mixed with how much water and ice and how large a profit you could make on refreshments, which group of girls would be flattered, have evening dresses and really show up to be ushers. For years she had done these things without thinking.

She couldn't very well teach all the tricks of direction in five days, but once she got hold of a script book she would mark it out so clearly that no one could go very wrong. She did get in a good deal of instruction such as:

"This is a walk line! Walk on that!"

"Here's what I mean by *build*—now BUILD!"

"Top that! Top it!"

She even taught Sister Consolata how to do a double take until she found her practicing it in the refectory, to the embarrassment of the reader at table.

Over and over she found herself saying, "Of course you can do it. You can do anything you're told to do. Just remember, no bottled drinks at the plays. Just paper cups. The boys can only douse each other with water and you have a mess, but they can't roll paper cups down the aisle. And be sure . . ."

So, thank God, she used up four days. The fifth day, which had to come, arrived.

Chapter 17

She had been afraid of the fifth day and had kept it mostly for herself. The early morning had been all right because she had been packing. There were not many things to go, once she had thrown out most of her old notes. Never need them again. Professors of Shakespeare and of poetic drama would have no use for these elementary devices that she had picked up through the years. Now she must get down to hours in the library and know all about the first folios and alternate readings. Stuff and bother. To her, Shakespeare had always been a good show. Good theatre.

Before the girls began to drop over in the afternoon, she slipped across the lawn side of the convent to the rectory, and knocked on the back door as she had so often done before, to get some permission or other from a reluctant pastor. She could hear him now, inside, pulling his collar on. It was a hot day and he would have to button his collar and that always put him in a bad mood. She didn't care.

He came to the door at last.

"So it's you, is it?" he said. "I might have known."

"Yes. It's me."

"Two o'clock in the afternoon! Didn't you ever hear of the civilized practice of the Roman siesta?"

"I came to say good-by. It was the only time I had."

"So we're not good enough for you here at St. Rita's."

"I didn't ask to be transferred, Monsignor," she said.

"And I'll bet you didn't ask to stay either."

"It isn't my place. I have to go where obedience sends me."

"Sure you do. But I know as much about your Holy Rule as you do. You're allowed to represent—that's what they call it—represent. Aren't you?"

Represent. That meant the right to inform Superiors of weighty reasons against carrying out their judgments. Why should she have represented? She had no weighty reasons except her own warm love of St. Rita's. What on earth did he mean?

"Why yes, Father. We can represent. But I haven't any case."

"Oh, you haven't? The good of this parish isn't any reason, is it? That never crossed your mind, did it? So it's your own choice, running off to the Cliffs. Well, good luck to you."

She wanted to cry out to him, "It isn't my choice! It's tearing the heart out of me." But if she did that, she would be being dramatic and it had been years since she had dared to be dramatic. They always accused her of it anyway.

To him she said, "Thank you, Monsignor. And thanks for everything you have given me here."

He cleared his throat. "You've got everything you wanted. I never gave in to a woman in my life the way I gave in to you. You've always gotten your own way. So, God bless you, and get on to your Cliffs."

He was a funny one, the Monsignor, she thought as she went back to the convent. It was true. He had always given in at the last. But she had had to fight him every inch of the way and many times she had thought that he was putting up an opposition for the sheer fun of it. Now this was a strange attitude of his, as if he really didn't want her to go.

Of course he did. He'd have his own way now, with nobody to oppose him. It would be all: "Yes, Monsignor. Whatever you wish, Monsignor. You're always right, Monsignor. What would you like us to do?" There was no spunk in any of the nuns left at St. Rita's, now that she and Drusilda were gone. Drusilda and herself. Funny that at last she should couple herself with Drusilda. Mother Drusilda. Her new Superior. Yet it was true; none of those who were left had any gumption.

And that is precisely what Monsignor Cooney was thinking as he unloosened his collar again and sat down in the armchair that was peculiarly his own.

Then there were some last good-bys. She was putting off the farewell to Mother Mount Carmel partially that it might be the last, partially because she was still disturbed and did not want to show it at their last meeting. For Mrs. Doyle had been right. Mother Mount Carmel could have kept her had she had a mind to. She could have fought for her. She was letting her go. Was the devotion and loyalty to be all on one side, on the subject's side?

Mrs. Doyle. She called Mrs. Doyle on the telephone but she could not reach her nor did Mrs. Doyle come around to the convent. She couldn't be that disturbed, could she? Yet her attitude gave Sister Gervaise a presentiment. Something was afoot.

She did not expect to hear from Mrs. Morrison, nor did she, but she felt a little slighted when even Rosemary did not drop by. The nine lepers. To come to say good-by, wasn't that the least she could have done? But then, why should she? Did she not know that Sister Gervaise had ranged herself in the camp of the enemy?

Maybe Joe Maguire hadn't intended to come around, but she rather thought he had. Boys could be so aggravatingly casual.

"Hi, Sister!" She heard his voice over the back fence as she was taking her last wimple down from the clothesline. He and Nick were there.

"Hello!"

They both grinned broadly. Nick! He had lost a front tooth!

"Not going to say good-by," Joe shouted at her. "No sense to it!"

"Good. But why no sense?"

"Going to see you every Thursday next year."

"How's that?"

"Guess you didn't know. I'm going to the sem next year in Sheraton. We get Thursdays off. I'll be over. Have some cokes for us."

Joe to the seminary! How could these things happen? It would be Nick next.

"That's wonderful! I'm so glad. I never dreamed . . ."

"Fooled you!"

"Indeed you did. And—and what about you, Nick?"

Nick grinned again. That missing front tooth! It made him look so different. "I'm going to work in a package store. Want any booze, let me know."

Good-by . . . good-by . . .

"Good-by, S'ter."

They were off. So it was Theresa, of course, who brought the final news, for if her mother was studiously unavailable,

Theresa was not. It was very casually, aggravatingly so, that Theresa dropped the news.

"Just to think!" Theresa said. "I'm going to be abandoned. There's Joe up at the sem . . ."

"So you know?"

"Oh sure. We're giving a party for him Tuesday." Naturally she was not brokenhearted. What did you expect? "And you're leaving, and that old Rosemary—she gets everything—she's going to have you in class again next year, and little old me will have to mark time for a whole year."

"Rosemary? I don't think so."

"Haven't you heard?"

"I don't get around much."

"Oh, Rosemary's going to the Cliffs!"

"I thought she had other plans."

"Her? Why, we all knew right along."

They probably did. The teenagers had known. Why had there been this tempest in a teapot among the oldsters? Maybe it would have been just as well to have asked one of Rosemary's contemporaries. Theresa, for instance. Funny, nobody had thought of that.

Should she ask how Rosemary felt about Joe now? Or how Theresa felt? She did not have to.

"Course, Joe's going away, that settled a lot of problems for most of us. You can see that."

"I certainly can. Just how did it settle you, for instance?"

"Me? Oh now—now I can concentrate on my career. And I will, Sister. You'll be proud of me!"

"I doubtless will. I am, Theresa. No matter what you do, I'll be proud of you." And Theresa probably wouldn't even have the lead in the class play. But she would have a career. Sister Gervaise at this moment was perfectly certain of that.

Her last mail had come. It was a letter from Margaret full of plans for what she was going to do after she came back from her honeymoon, and how she and Jim would take Sister Gervaise and Sister Consolata out for a ride in the country some fine day. That would be nice. Also, it would never happen.

Then Sister Gervaise began her own final farewells. She went first to Mother Mount Carmel's room and, not allowing herself time to think, rapped. There was no answer, but she was almost sure she heard something stirring within. She waited a moment. It might be the breeze in the curtain. She thought not, though. And, as she waited, she resolved to tell Mother everything: how she had been rebellious, how she had been suspicious, even of her, and of how she was going, not in any spirit of joy in doing God's will, but with a heavy load upon her. She could, she must talk to Mother just as she had done as a novice. It was good to have her here, even for this one moment—even if it were not to be for a year. She rapped again.

Sister Emily came down the corridor then, and paused, wondering if charity were a sufficient reason for breaking silence, and deciding, with some heroism, that in this case it was.

"Didn't you hear?" she asked. "Mother Mount Carmel just got called away. It was quite sudden, they tell me. She had to take Mother Dolorosa to the hospital. They think maybe it was a stroke."

She said no more. Emily departed, and now the corridor looked bare indeed. There was nothing here. Nothing to say good-by to.

Sister Gervaise went out for a last good-by to the convent places. She did not go over to the auditorium. She knew that by heart anyway. But she looked across the asphalt pavement to the basement door of the school. It was hot today, but she felt cold, seeing it. Many a snowy night she had hurried across from there to the convent.

She turned then toward Lady's kennel.

"Lady," she called. She could not see the dog, but then she spied her, lying in the shade. Lady did not come to her, but lay there, out of the heat, languidly. She had always loved Lady, but Lady had never attached herself to Gervaise as she had to Sister Inez.

"You might at least say good-by," she said. Lady's tail beat a little on the dust and subsided. "All right. If that's the way you want it." She scratched the dog's ear and departed.

She went over then to the new grotto where the statue that she always called Our Lady of the Transition stood. For a long time, while the light from the evening sun fell around her, she remained there. In this peace she let the sorrow of her parting from this place come to her again. After her first rebellion she had filled these last few days so that she would feel nothing. Now there was no rebellion, only an acceptance of the necessity of leaving, of doing what she was told.

It was so that Sister Consolata found her.

"I hoped you were out here," the little nun said. "I came to say good-by. And to thank you for everything."

"I haven't done anything. I only helped myself."

"No. That isn't so. You gave yourself for me when I, in your place, would have been all broken up about leaving St. Rita's. I didn't even accept my new job very well, did I? You'll always be an inspiration to me."

"Me? That's a good one."

"Yes, you. You don't want to go, do you?"

"Of course not. All my life, so far, has been here."

✧ 223

"But you never thought of doing anything else, did you, except going?"

"Naturally. What else could I do? But inwardly, you should have heard me growl."

Sister Consolata looked at her intently. She was very young in years but in that moment in the twilight she had grown inscrutably old and wise.

"I never heard," Sister Consolata said, "that the Rule told us not to feel things. They didn't teach us in the novitiate that we would never have temptations or that we wouldn't be hurt or that ideas of injustice and self-pity wouldn't cross our minds. They just told us that we should fight them down and go right ahead. But when my time came, I didn't do it very well. You did."

"Yes? But you don't know. I didn't. Really."

"Yes, you did. You didn't even know it. You began to think about somebody else. Me. I'll never forget it."

Sister Consolata reached out and holding Sister Gervaise's hands, kissed her on both cheeks.

"Thanks," she said.

It made Sister Gervaise ashamed. I'm glad she can't see inside me. I'm not like she thinks. Just today I allowed myself vindictive thoughts about the Monsignor. And he has been good to me, I think. Yesterday it was Mr. MacGill. And since the status came I have avoided Mother Mount Carmel until it was too late to see her. Yes, I did, because I kept thinking, underneath, that she might have kept me here if she had wanted to. And through all that . . .

There was only one thing. She really had never considered putting obstacles in Mother Provincial's way, and honestly, that had been part of her reason for not seeing Mother Mount Carmel. Only part, she knew, but a good part.

224 ✍

She had rejected the pastor's suggestion of representation as an absurd fancy. From the beginning she had known that she would go to the Cliffs, and that was that.

"Our Lady of the Transition," she said, turning to the statue, "I have learned the first lesson of obedience all right. I go where I am told. And the first lesson of detachment; physically, I give things up. Now if you are kind to me, you can teach me the other lessons. The gladness, the willingness they talk about. The eagerness to do the real will of Superiors even when you have a chance to do your own. I just haven't got that far yet."

She had turned away toward the house when the portress hastened out after her.

"The Pope wants to speak to you on the phone!"

"Who?"

"Well, it practically is. It's Reverend Mother Provincial."

Now what?

She heard the voice on the other end of the wire, way off in Sheraton.

"Sister Gervaise? This is Mother Bernardine. I suppose you are all packed to come here?"

"Yes, Reverend Mother."

"Then unpack." There was a little ice in the voice. "I discover that you are indispensable there."

"But I'm already . . ."

"I have on my desk two letters. One is a long list of names headed by a Mrs. Doyle. You know of that, of course. She informs me that you do."

"But I don't. I never sanctioned such a thing."

"She makes that quite clear. But she also says you did not forbid her to proceed."

"How could I? I had no idea she meant it."

~ 225

"Do you or do you not want to stay at St. Rita's?"

"Well, I—of course I want to do what you—I mean, suppose I did say . . ."

"I gather that you told this Mrs. Doyle that you wanted to stay. But all that could be overlooked. Lay interference. But take this other letter now . . ."

"Another one?"

"Yes. It's more important. It's from Monsignor Cooney. He says, in rather vigorous terms, that you have not only built up the plays at St. Rita's and—and—made a lot of money, but that you're the best teacher there. And he adds that, as a matter of fact, I quote: 'She's the only live woman in the parish. I didn't object when you took Drusilda away with you, God knows, but three in one year is too much. In fact, if you keep this up I'm thinking of bringing in the . . .' He names another Order."

"Monsignor Cooney? I thought he didn't like me. I thought he wanted me out of here."

Now the voice was dry. "He mentions that, too, Sister. Here it is. 'Don't think for a moment I ask this because of my personal interest in Sister Gervaise. We haven't agreed on anything since she came here. But she puts up a good fight. I need someone around to,' I quote, 'to keep me hopping.' You have quite a reputation with the pastor, Sister Gervaise." A silence increased the long-distance toll. "So I have decided that in this case I will yield. You had better unpack."

"Yes, Mother . . . Mother? Where do you want me to be?"

"I wanted you at Marycliff. I need somebody to teach Shakespeare as if he didn't originally appear in an annotated edition. I also need a few more degrees in the catalogue. But I suppose I'll have to forget all that."

I wish I hadn't been told! I could have made a real sacrifice. Real obedience. Now I know the reasons, my sacrifice is no good.

"Mother—may I come to the Cliffs?"

"I don't see how."

"I'll see Mrs. Doyle. She has a personal reason. Her daughter was to have had the lead in the play. I'll get Sister Consolata to cast her and then Mrs. Doyle will be happy."

"And the pastor?"

Sister Gervaise laughed. "I've always managed to handle him. We might as well end the way we've been going. With a good fight. He says he loves it. So I'll go out with a bang, not a whimper."

She could hear Mother Bernardine's chuckle at the other end. "I don't approve of that at all, Sister. But we'll see you at the Cliffs tomorrow."

"Yes, Mother."

"Sister?"

"Yes, Mother."

"Do you really want to come here?"

"Yes, Mother."

"Supernaturally speaking?"

"Yes, Mother."

"And naturally?"

"No, Mother."

And Sister Gervaise was not sure, but she thought that she heard Mother Provincial say, as she hung up the receiver, "You're all right, Sister Gervaise."

The Lively Arts of Sister Gervaise

By JOHN L. BONN

SOMEHOW OR OTHER, no matter how hard she tried to stay in the background, Sister Gervaise always seemed to find herself in the center of the stage. Perhaps it was because her father was in the theatre; maybe the fact that she was the "Dramatic Nun" at St. Rita's High School had something to do with it. Or it might have been her devotion to the Cause—to art, liturgy, drama, music. Whatever it was, Sister Gervaise was involved in everything from a parish family's domestic troubles to an inter-conventual controversy on art.

Father Bonn has written a spirited novel in which Sister Gervaise's championship of such things as abstract madonnas, Gregorian chant and the cultural benefits of T. S. Eliot and Henri Ghéon on the high-school stage lead to unforeseen complications. Her artful way with human problems surrounds her with a gallery of people, distinct, personable and as engaging as the nun around whom they revolve.

But Sister Gervaise, despite her students' firm belief that she is the next thing to the Oracle at Delphi, has her own problems too, and in working them out she learns to laugh at her own mistakes and deepens her understanding of what the convent Rule demands of her. When the pastor, Monsignor Cooney, calls Sister Gervaise "the only live woman in the parish," one feels he has good reason to think so, and feels too that the dauntless "Dramatic Nun" is one of those rare characterizations who will win an enduring place on the fictional stage.